W9-ANP-752

The Ming Legacy

by Carol DeGrange

Cover: Phillip Buttermore

Express Press

THE MING LEGACY

FIRST EDITION
Copyright © 2003 by
Carol DeGrange

Library of Congress Catalog Card Number: 2003103243

ISBN 0-7880-2084-6
PRINTED IN U.S.A.

To my husband and my
best friend,
DON HOBSON

The spring sunlight angled through the
glass persistently, outlining each object in
the train compartment with a golden border.

Outside, the Chinese countryside was quickening;
the air carried the moist, pungent smell of newly
worked earth in through the open window.

Another smell, cloyingly sweet, came from
the body which lay draped across the window table.
One arm was flung over the man's head so that his
lifeless fingers tapped the table edge in rhythm with
the vibrations of the train wheels.

He had come a long way from home to die.

Characters

Long Qiong, the university waiban and the owner of the Ming vase

Long Wenshi, Qiong's younger brother

Jing Lingzi, Qiong's mother

Chan Lumei, Qiong's wife

Long Qi, Qiong's ancestor who was first given the Ming vase

Rachel Toussant, an older American women teaching in Jilin

Melanie Hazen, also an American teaching in Jilin

Paul Solomon, a male American teaching in Jilin

Laura Mance, another teacher in Jilin

Frank Li, Laura's Chinese friend

Sidney Mance, Laura's husband who owns an art gallery in the U.S.

Claire Lucas, an American-Chinese woman who works for Sidney Mance

George Kim, a Chinese-American who also works for Sidney Mance

Lu Xing, a detective on the Jilin-Yanji train

other minor characters

Chapter 1

Jilin City, (Manchuria) China

1966

The noise was enough to drive a person mad. As the familiar ache settled into the socket of Long Qiong's right eye and began to spread down the side of his face, he gave up trying to read and rested his elbows on the table, holding his throbbing head in his hands.

The gongs and shouted slogans of the Red Guards who paraded up and down the streets outside his window seemed to have no end. The crowd made up in energy what they had lost in reason. To Long Qiong, the pain that he was experiencing now seemed like a metaphor for the experiences of his country — periodic spasms of intense anguish, inexplicable in their origins but constantly hovering at the edge of consciousness ready to strike at random.

Long's mother, Jing Lingzi, peered anxiously into his bedroom through the beaded doorway screen.

"Long Qiong, are you all right?" she asked quietly. She knew he wasn't but she always hoped. The guilt she felt when he was ill was coupled with a nagging irritation.

"Why can't he be healthier?" she would ask herself as she looked at his puffy eyes and pinched white face to gauge how bad this episode was going to be. "He's so different from Wenshi," she thought. Again, she felt guilty making comparisons. Long Qiong was plain; his physique was slight. But his younger brother, Wenshi — now there was a beautiful face and a body full of vigor. Just to look at him brought pleasure. But Wenshi's spirit, ah ... his spirit ... that was not so good. He was possessed of a meanness that his mother was reluctant to acknowledge. It was there nonetheless. Yes, Wenshi and Qiong were certainly opposites — so strange that two sons could be so different. Jing Lingzi had to admit that Qiong

9

made up in spirit for what he lacked in physical appearance. His spirit was rare; he was a highly moral person with an intellect to be reckoned with. Many of the qualities he possessed were those that she had also loved in his father.

Jing Lingzi moved quietly to the window, pulled the piece of cloth which served as a curtain across the opening, and patted it into place so that even the smallest shaft of sunlight would not enter. Then she tugged gently on Long Qiong's sleeve.

"Come, lie down," she said. "I'll fix a cool cloth for your head."

"Oh, the damnable noise," he complained. "This pandemonium in the streets is insane." The pain in his head made him irritable and intensely angry with himself for his inability to control it. However, he was even more angry with his countrymen. The people *were* mad, truly out of their minds. They had created a new religion, and the name of their new god was Mao Zedong. How could these young people stand to repeat the same phrases over and over? Surely they must be hoarse. And how could Mao bear to hear his own name praised in such mindless repetition?

Long lowered himself carefully onto the bed. When he had these migraine attacks, his mind invariably raced instead of giving him the peace he needed. Inevitably, he found himself worrying over his past and his future like a dog chewing on a meatless bone. He knew that in 1946, when he was just an infant, the people had begun to hope again as the Japanese invaders and then finally the Soviets, had withdrawn from the area. By the time the Chinese Nationalists arrived in Manchuria, the leaders in the new Chinese Communist Party had already established a strong base here, especially in the rural areas.

Qiong learned from what his parents had said that most people welcomed the revolutionary ideas of the young Mao Zedong and had held little regard for Chiang Kai-shek who led the Nationalist Chinese Army. Manchuria had been devastated by the Japanese. Mao gave the people hope and purpose; he was one of them, not one of the upper class like Chiang Kai-shek. Now, that purpose had soured for all but the youngest, the newly declared *Red Guards*... his little (*xiao*) brother and his brother's friends. Yet almost all of

10

the people went along with Mao's dictates, not just the young. Therein lay the madness.

Qiong despaired of his future. Ever since he could remember, his greatest desire had been to be a scholar, to study, to help form the new China by understanding the past and using that knowledge. But of what use was study in times such as these? As a young intellectual, he was now part of the hated class of scholars which the communists called the *stinking ninth*. He represented those despised elements which were being destroyed by a crazy ideology that sought to re-invent everything by wiping out the past.

The lack of power Long felt was demoralizing. What could he do about *Xiao* Wenshi? As the elder brother and the head of the household since his father's death, Long Qiong was responsible for his family. That responsibility weighed heavily on him; hence his often dour demeanor; hence the mustache which was an attempt to echo his father's strength.

Long Qiong was constantly mystified as to how he and his brother could be so different. When he looked into the mirror, he saw an austere-faced man whose protruding eyes gave him a perpetually surprised look. His friends told him that his mustache, groomed in the manner of his father's, made him seem definitely sinister. He knew, however, that it saved him from appearing totally naive. His was certainly not a face to inspire confidence, yet those closest to him knew him to be completely trustworthy.

Long Wenshi, his younger brother, had just turned sixteen and was already a compellingly handsome man whose flashing reckless smile was irresistible to women and charismatic to his fellows. Only those who lived with him knew that his carefree recklessness overlaid a less carefree penchant for gratuitous violence. Qiong was certain that Wenshi's voice was joined in with the din outside.

The three, Long Qiong, Long Wenshi and their mother, Jing Lingzi, lived now in two small rooms in the city of Jilin which was in the far Northeast Manchu part of China. The two brothers slept in one room while their mother occupied the other kitchen/main sitting room/bedroom. Most households were a cramped, uneasy meld of conflicting forces in these hard years of the 1960's. Their

11

household was no exception. Long Qiong knew that his mother was devastated by the lack of respect Wenshi showed her. His lack of deference extended to his elder brother and any other person or thing truly worthy of respect.

The Confucian codes which had sought to maintain order for well over two thousand years seemed suddenly obsolete. Today it was "get rid of the four olds: old thought, old customs, old culture and old morals." When he remonstrated with Little Wenshi about his late night activities and his failure to study, *Xiao* Wenshi just laughed as though he possessed the most amusing secret. "I don't need to know that outdated rubbish. My comrades and I are young soldiers of China helping to build a new country. You should take your nose out of your decadent books and try to develop some different skills, perhaps farming. You may someday have need of them." After such an outburst, Wenshi usually flung himself out the door and did not return until near daybreak.

Long Qiong often slept fitfully after these exchanges. In a recurring dream, he was racing through the snow covered forests near Jilin with an urgent message for some unnamed person. His heart was an undulating mass of worms in his chest. He could sense that a huge Manchurian tiger lurked nearby measuring his progress, the ice tipped claws in its massive paws involuntarily contracting in anticipation. As a child, he had witnessed the capture of such a beast and even then had known that an amoral menace of such strength could never be truly confined.

He jerked awake at the sounds of his brother getting into bed.

"Eh, a bad dream elder brother?" Then a soft laugh, "The Buddhists will be having bad dreams too."

Long Qiong coughed then whispered, "What, what do you mean?"

"Remember the Guardian of the West on Beishan Mountain, my brother? Well, he no longer guards the West." Another soft laugh turned almost immediately into light snoring.

Long Qiong lay staring into the pale light as morning approached. The tiger *was* close by. He must do something to protect his mother. He studied the cracks on the ceiling pondering what to do. It was only when he heard his mother leave for the morning marketing that he came to a decision. His mother must leave Jilin. Perhaps she would agree to stay with his aunt in the remote eastern part of the province. Having made that decision, he slept lightly in the early hours of daylight.

Later that morning, when his mother returned from her daily marketing, she was agitated and pale.

"Long Qiong, the most awful thing— during the night the Buddhist statues at Beishan Temple were smashed—all of them! I don't understand. We thought things would be better, but now it is even worse. Before, the Japanese were destroying us. Now we destroy ourselves." She began to weep, something she had not permitted herself even at his father's funeral.

Qiong tried to calm her, but he, himself, was convinced that things would only get worse in the days to come. He lifted her chin so that she was looking directly at him and then spoke with all the authority he could muster, "Mother, it is time for you to visit Auntie Xu. Things are too chaotic here. It will be better there. Remember just last week you said you worried so much about her taking care of the ginseng farm all alone. She is your older sister and could certainly use your help. Surely, in that remote place the Red Guards will be too lazy to climb the Changbai Mountains. I know you've been thinking about going there."

"Oh, Qiong," she began to cry again, "How did you know that I wanted to leave here? I have been wanting to get away from this place; it would be so peaceful with my sister, and ..." She paused, fear and anger playing across her face. She looked at Qiong with anguish. "Jilin has become such a lawless place. The country side would be calm, but I'm afraid for *Xiao* Wenshi... Who would take care of him?"

"Hush, mother. You know Wenshi doesn't listen to either of us anymore. Do you actually think for one minute that your being here will affect what he does or what happens to him? Don't worry; he is clever. He'll be all right no matter what happens, and I'll watch out for him the best I can."

Even in his concern for his mother, her concentration always on Wenshi exasperated him — jealousy — of his brother? — a

13

shameful emotion he would not permit in himself. His countenance softened towards her as her eyes teared over. She wiped them quickly and gave a wry smile as though she could read his mind."My worthy son, perhaps you are right. I have been thinking about Auntie Xu for some time. Yes, I'd enjoy being with her, and she does need me. You know she's ten years older than I am — not young anymore. But I would miss you very much. It's a time to be exceedingly careful. These days are becoming treacherous." She embraced him quickly and smiled up at him as she traced his moustache with her finger.

"I'm fine now," she said. "Leave me alone for a while. I must decide what I need to do."

Several hours later she called Long Qiong from his studies to tell him that she had decided to go. She held up several lists saying, "Here are my instructions on running the household while I'm gone."Qiong could barely keep from smiling when he saw the detailed lists she had drawn up. Every possible contingency had been covered.

"Mother, I *am* a grown man, and a capable one too; however, if it will make you happy, I will consult your lists daily. You may picture me rising every morning to read your lists before I begin my day."

Both of them broke out laughing at the thought of this.

"Now I'll start my packing," Jing Lingzi, said. She paused abruptly with a look of intense concentration on her face. "Qiong," she said, "Before I make this trip, we must first take a short journey together."

"What kind of a journey? Where?"

"No, no questions now; you will soon see. Right now I must pack. I'll explain as we travel. For now, I can only say that it is most important," and with a mysterious sidelong glance at him, "... yes, you are old enough now to share a great family secret. But we mustn't tell your brother. He's too young."

Long Qiong was tempted to add, "And too unreliable," but he knew it would only hurt his mother to have him say what she must be thinking.

She continued, " We'll leave in the morning after Wenshi has gone out on his *important errands*. We can be back before evening. He needn't even know we've been gone."

The next morning was crisp and stunningly bright, but his mother's eyes looked even more brilliant than the sky. She raced around with a youthful air preparing a basket in which, miracle of miracles, lay two hard-boiled eggs. It also contained cold rice, *jiao-zi* dumplings, chopsticks, a thermos of tea and a mysterious long object wrapped in dark blue shirting material.

It was like the games she had played with him when he was a child. She smiled with a mischievous grin. He knew what she must have looked like as a child herself, spirited, strong and full of laughter.

"Now we are ready," she said as she hid the container in the cupboard. "Why don't you read to me while we wait? *Xiao* Wenshi will awaken soon and begin his busy day. Read Li Bai perhaps. Surely, even Chairman Mao knows we can't think of production schedules constantly. Life for our country has never been easy. Fortunately, our poets have kept us sane."

"Amazing," he thought, "I haven't really known my mother. She has never seemed to have any political awareness, but here she has been thinking, always thinking."

The two, reader and listener, presented a rather sedate appearance as Wenshi, finally out of bed, shot by with the air of an important, busy man out to do serious things. Something about the scene made him turn back from the door with a puzzled glance. He looked at them as though they were a kind of alien species, then shrugged and went on his way. Immediately, Long Qiong and Jing Lingzi set out for the train station.

Jing Lingzi, was clearly in charge on this expedition. All Qiong could do was follow, silently marveling at her incredible energy.

After they had settled themselves on the train, his mother became serious. She asked, "Qiong, what do you remember of the Ming Dynasty and how it fell?"

Long looked at her quizzically. "Most things." He didn't see the point of her question. Jing Lingzi read his face and with a flutter of her hand continued, "My question isn't idle. It's part of what you must know. Our trip has to do with our ancestor, Long Qi, and an event that took place in his life shortly after the fall of the Ming Dynasty. It's all part of a strange story."

"Ah," replied Qiong, "He's the one whose portrait hangs on our wall. When I was a child, it frightened me terribly. Did you know that? He seemed so remote, like a god who always watched us. And his face ..." Long laughed. "I would try to get him to look at me to tell me about himself, but his eyes were so forbidding and his face in the portrait was so faded that it made me think of death. I would lose my nerve and turn away."

"Perhaps you didn't try hard enough, my son. He was once a man like you. I think ... he ... our ancestors do watch over us. It is not so strange that we look to them for wisdom. We are in the middle of our search; they have completed theirs.

Our family has been more fortunate than many. Since the time of Long Qi, we've been blessed. And because of him, we have a remarkable legacy which came to us in 1644 just after the Ming Dynasty ended."

"A legacy ... of what?"

"I will show you soon — when we visit your father's grave. As you know, the Ming Dynasty began in 1368 when the Han Chinese finally gathered the strength to overthrow the Mongols who had ruled them for the past 89 years. Throughout the Ming dynasty many strong emperors were able to expand their rule to cover wide areas of Asia."

Qiong nodded. His mother was being pedantic, but he was nevertheless delighted. He had never had a conversation like this with her. Their roles seemed to be reversed; she was now the teacher-scholar, and he was the student.

"Yes," he agreed, "it was a powerful dynasty. I suppose it must have seemed to them that such a vast empire would go on forever."

"Exactly, and of course, in many ways, the emperors cut themselves off from reality when they established the *Forbidden City* as their walled residence making it a separate city in the heart of Peking."

"No commoners allowed," Qiong added scornfully. He was slightly embarrassed by the modern egalitarianism his comment

16

reflected. He believed strongly in justice but not in the leveling to the lowest common denominator which the communists required of everyone. He certainly didn't want to sound like Wenshi.

He continued, "But I would guess that, to some extent, reigning from such a mysterious realm served to increase the emperor's power and importance in the eyes of the average person rather than limit it."

"Certainly, but eventually that isolation took its toll. How could an emperor know what his people needed when he lived such a privileged life?" Jing Lingzi sighed, "Still, the *Forbidden City* must have been a splendid place then. Just think, a magnificent city within a city where only the most noble and the most talented walked. The silks ... the jade, beautiful paintings, jewels—"

"And," interrupted Long Qiong, "the common people living their mean existence and dying outside those walls."

"Of course," answered his mother, "I wasn't saying it was just, but ..." She paused for a moment caught in her private thoughts. Then she said in a rush, "I would so like to have seen the *Forbidden City* just once the way it was, not as the museum it is now with hundreds of people tramping through having their pictures taken beside the guardian lions, but as it must have been on a quiet evening with the setting sun outlining the roof on the Hall of the Golden Throne and the sounds of a flute coming from one of the gardens." She gave Long a shy smile. "Does that sound too foolish?"

"No, mother, I understand how you feel about beautiful things. I love them too. Unfortunately, in China so much of our beauty was built on the backs of people who lived in ugliness."

"Yes, I suppose you're right. That was especially true at the end of the Ming Dynasty. The imperial bureaucracy had paralyzed the central government so that finances for military manpower were scarce."

"I remember from the accounts of that time that lack of currency was one of the major sources of unrest among the people," replied Qiong. "Many of the soldiers had not been paid for months, and it was the soldiers who made that splendid seclusion of the court possible."

"Ah, but if you recall, it was also a soldier who hastened the end," his mother shot back.

"You mean Wu Sangui, the general who opened his garrison to our ancestors, the Manchus?"

"Yes, Wu Sangui — a complex man. There are so many myths about him that no one knows what really happened, but our ancestor, Long Qi, was closer to him than most. Long Qi was his personal aide."

Long Qiong was beginning to understand where their conversation was heading. His, ancestor, Long Qi, must have had special knowledge of Wu Sangui that their personal family history alone had preserved.

Jing Lingzi continued, " Many of the stories paint Wu as a traitor, but you must remember that the politics of the time were extremely unstable. There was much jealousy among the few strong ones at the top who scrambled for power under the very nose of the emperor; some of those men wrote the histories. A general like Wu had no time to record his own actions.

When the Ming Dynasty fell, Wu was stationed at Shanhaiguan which was a strategic pass between China and Manchuria, supposedly to protect the capital from the possible invasion of our ancestors, the Manchus, from the Northeast. Because of the monetary difficulties which were destabilizing the country, Li Zicheng, a rebel from the South, found enough support to launch an assault on Peking and the Forbidden City. The story is that the father of Wu Sangui was captured, tortured and executed by this rebel. Also, Wu's concubine was tortured and then returned to him. At some point, the emperor sent word to Wu to return with his troops to defend the capital. Some historians say that he didn't get the message; others say that he knew that he didn't have enough troops to prevail and ignored the summon; still others believe that he wanted revenge for the death of his father and could only get that revenge by joining his forces with the strength of the Manchu army. Whatever the reasons, Wu did open his garrison to the Manchus and join their forces."

Qiong became excited. "And you say that Long Qi knew him well."

18

"Yes, the story that has been passed down in our family is one that Long Qi told. He had watched Wu; he had listened to him and he felt that he knew Wu's thoughts."

"We are visiting father's grave, aren't we?"

Jing Lingzi nodded. "Yes."

"And that has something to do with Long Qi?"

Again Qiong's mother indicated yes, but before he could ask more, the train was pulling to a stop at a small village to the north-west of Changchun.

The two hour train ride seemed to have taken only minutes. When Qiong and his mother got off, he expected her to bargain with someone for a cart ride into the countryside, but she wasn't inclined to do so.

"Today we walk," she said. "It is fine weather and the exercise will do us good. I want you to remember every moment of this day so that you can tell your son, the son you will have someday."

Qiong didn't protest. If she was prepared to walk an eight *li* round trip, he certainly could; however, later, it was with some relief that they finally arrived near the mounded graves where she instructed him to spread the cloth out under the pines.

"While we eat," she said, " I will tell you Long Qi's story." In this setting of absolute quiet broken only by his mother's voice and the droning of insects, Qiong heard about the relationship between his ancestor, Long Qi, and the famous Ming general, Wu Sangui, as though it were told through Wu's voice.

The sunlight filtered through the pines and caused the stones it hit to sparkle. With the grave mounds ranged behind them in peaceful community, Qiong had a feeling of time stretched and then compressed, a suspension of reality he was to feel again in his life when time seemed to stop to let history catch up with the present. Jing Lingzi told the story of a particular night hundreds of years ago as though she were a medium seeing inside the mind of Wu Sangui himself. The precision of detail was so fine that Long Qiong felt transported to those very moments in the camp northeast of Peking.

Chapter 2

The Story of Wu Sangui

May 17, 1644

Wu watched as the two figures, silhouetted against the crackling flames which enveloped the *Forbidden City* moved heavily toward the hill. He could not erase that scene from his mind. Strange, that he could so clearly visualize an event he had not witnessed.

In this vivid re-creation, *his* emperor, accompanied by a retainer, moved with more deliberate purpose than he had ever shown throughout the long duty years of his reign. Wu could see this weary form reach the base of Coal Hill behind the palace complex and turn to gaze in astonishment and regret at the picture of carnage which was spread behind him. The emperor's private world where he had reigned supreme was turning to ashes and he, the Son of Heaven, could do nothing.

This Chongzhen emperor, under whom Wu had served, had been an unexceptional human being imprisoned by an extraordinarily rigid system. It was senseless to believe that anyone, let alone this mortal man, could fulfill that impossible expectation to incarnate the ideal as the Son of Heaven.

It was reported to Wu that the emperor had written a final message in his own blood on that April night which so frequently inhabited Wu's vision:

My virtue is small, and therefore I have incurred the
anger of heaven and rebels have captured my capital.

Wu, saw the scene as though it were in front of his eyes. Zhu Youjian, the Chongzhen emperor, removed the girdle from his robe, patiently and carefully fashioned it into a noose, and with the help of his retainer, fastened it to a nearby tree. Then, pausing only a moment to adjust it around his neck, the emperor stepped out from the log on which he was standing into the empty air. Wu's chest constricted. Lights burst in his head at the image of the gentle

21

swing, swing, swing of the body so peaceful against a backdrop of screams and voraciously dancing flames.

It was not merely a dream; it was Wu's fate to have such a horror indelibly etched into his mind where it intruded again and again, a grey nightmare not confined to night, an insistently creeping curse against which there was no defense. Had the moon been visible that night, or had Wu placed one in his imagined landscape as an impassive presence, remote from the frenzy below it? The unknown detail was, for some perplexing reason, an insistently nagging worry.

Shaking his head vigorously, Wu willed his mind away from the past into the present moment. A trusted general did not give flight to his imagination. Wars had more horrors than any one consciousness could bear to retain. He laughed at himself. *Trusted*? — No, no. Now, no longer the supreme general of the Ming emperor, he was instead a *valuable*, but closely watched general in the Manchu army having defected when defense of the empire was no longer viable. Some might call him a traitor. In moments of anger toward himself, that choice seemed perfectly justified. The Ming emperor had been floundering. The imperial armies were too weak, even with Wu Sangui's expertise, to maintain the empire against the onslaught of well organized rebels intent on overthrowing the government. Nor could Wu have repelled the Manchus who were advancing on the capital from the Northeast. He considered himself to be an honorable man but not a suicidal one. Making the decision to collaborate with the enemy had been a practical way to survive and a means of retaining the power to avenge the horrible death of his father.

When Wu had learned that Li Zicheng and his rebels who were besieging the capital had kidnaped his father and his concubine, Wu dampened his imagination with anger. When a messenger brought the news of his father's death by torture, Wu forbade the man to speak of the details. He could not afford to listen. Instead, he plotted the next move of his troops with precision, knowing that being a grieving son and a successful general were mutually exclusive, and only a successful general could avenge that death. A general was above emotion; a general was pragmatic; a general survived.

The decision had been made. The worst time should be over. Why, now then, when sleep came, was it accompanied always by such enervating dreams? Dreams of his emperor — dreams of his father— dreams of his concubine— each full of horror and guilt ; they allowed no rest. When morning came, he awoke feeling exhaustion eating at his bones. Now that his father was dead and beyond the pain of the most ingenious devices of his torturers, Wu found that the facts that he had forbidden the messenger to speak of haunted him, becoming all the scenes of torture that he had ever witnessed. A man who had night terrors would not long retain his powers. These fantasies must not continue — must not.

As a general, Wu had always been a loyal, unfaltering arm of the emperor. Ah, but when loyalty to the father or to the emperor was mutually exclusive, how does one decide? The emperor had been pathetically weak, surrounded by sycophants who could not smell the danger at their very walls. Was it not, then, morally right to disobey, to choose one's own destiny, to be on the side of the victors?

Wu's very pragmatism had placed him here in another army as a general for the Manchus from the Northeast. He was no longer Zhu Youjian's man. Dead emperors did not need live men.

Still, what did these recurring dreams about his emperor say? Was he in fact a traitor or merely a cleverly expedient man who was now positioned to avenge his father's death? It was certain that his troops, along with the Manchu vanguard, would crush the rebel leader, Li Zicheng, and drive his followers out of Peking, but the Ming succession had died that April night with the death of *his* emperor in the *Forbidden City* at the hill of Wu's dreams, and something intrinsically vital had also died within the general, Wu Sangui.

Restless and weary, Wu surveyed his quarters, his eyes automatically seeking out the one thing which had previously given him such great satisfaction. Though tied to his ambiguous past, it held no ambiguity. What a small perfect thing! A small vase, exquisite in its vigor and execution. Two five-clawed red dragons exhaled curling scrolls of fire onto a pale mustard-yellow background. The vase was ringed top and bottom with a border of stylized clouds as strongly formed as the dragons themselves. Its small box-case of padded red silk stood beside it, for it was only at night that he removed this remarkable gift. It remained hidden during the day. Now the nightly ritual had become a compulsive torture.

The day the emperor had presented the vase to him, Wu's pride had been immeasurable. It symbolized the honor and esteem with which the emperor had regarded Wu and had, consequently, been a gift of enormous value even beyond its intrinsic perfection. On that day of honor, no one could ever have believed that he, Wu Sangui, one of the most highly regarded generals in the empire, would one day defect to the Manchus. Fate made seemingly impossible events possible and caused the humans who were its playthings untold anguish. If someone had foretold Wu what his future would bring, he would have chosen death then rather than what he would have considered dishonor. But events also have a way of qualifying people's reactions to them. He would never have the certainty that his choice was correct no matter how many sleepless nights he wrestled with the question. However, he knew that either choice meant that he could not live the days which followed without strong regrets. The vase mutely rebuked him, but he could not destroy it. That would be sacrilege. Still, the sight of it occasioned his most debilitating introspection and threatened him with unbearable remorse. Yet his need to torment himself by looking at it had become a nightly obsession. Perhaps it was what precipitated his dreams.

A scuffing sound caused Wu to turn to the entryway. His aide, Long Qi, stood hesitantly in the doorway.

"Come in. Sit. What are you doing up so late?"

"Your excellency, I saw your light and thought you might be in need of something."

"Perhaps you are right. A little less solitude and a little more conversation is what I do need. Tell me, Long, do you think often of your family? Where are they? Talk to me about them."

Long Qi looked puzzled. He replied carefully. "Surely, sir, with so much of great consequence to consider, you cannot truly be interested in the trivial details of my life."

"On the contrary. My mind is numbed by a mountain of sweeping plans. I need to hear about the ordinary to restore my belief in it."

With the flush of a self-conscious school boy, Long Qi began to speak. Soon his memories and attachments overcame his clumsiness, and he was speaking to Wu with a passionate openness about his family members. Their loves and quarrels became a soothing tale for Wu, and Long's simplicity restored a sense of serenity to the night.

"What a clever person Prince Dorgon is," reflected Wu, "to give me an aid such as Long Qi." It made sense that Long would have been instructed to report Wu's actions to the Prince who was the actual leader of the Manchu forces. And, of course, the Prince would know that Wu would expect such surveillance as a naturally prudent way to ensure his loyalty, given his status as a recently defecting general. What was so clever was that Long Qi was an intelligent but not a duplicitous person. He was most likable. That in itself was disarming. True, he was a Manchu, not a Han, but Wu knew he was a man of honor.

Wu had often fought beside Long Qi in battle. Long was an excellent, brave soldier who kept his head. He did not flinch from killing his enemy. But he took no great pleasure in it as did some of Wu's most seasoned warriors who lost their reason as blood-lust turned them into ravaging animals rather than calculating soldiers. Even in the press of battle, Long Qi was aware of his comrades. During a moment of carelessness, Wu, himself, had been the beneficiary of Long's alertness. As Wu was pulling his sword from the body of an enemy he had just slain, the whinny of a horse made him spin around. He was frozen by the ferocious face of the rider whose sword was raised over him for the killing blow. Before Wu could move, Long's sword cleanly severed the arm of the rider. Wu was drenched in blood, but it was not his own. He owed his life to Long Qi.

Wu thought intently about this constant companion he had been assigned. He was glad of his company. The lulling sound of Long's voice served as a backdrop sharpening Wu's other perceptions. Shadows cast by the glow of his oil lamp flickered and made strange shapes out of ordinary things. The fresh breeze brought snatches of sound from his soldiers, swelling and fading with the shifts of the wind. Wu sighed. The ferment of each day's events made the nights even more precious.

"...and so yes, I miss them greatly, especially my youngest daughter who is just this month four years old." Long Qi finished speaking and again became self-conscious. He lowered his head and gave a small, self-deprecating smile.

"Certainly, a truly good man," Wu thought. "Most men would think only of themselves and then of their sons. Their companions in battle would be forgotten. The daughter would be forgotten, an expendable and burdensome entity."

Wu looked again at the vase and contemplated his past. What was done was done. It was time to move beyond his regrets. A sudden impulse seized him, a solution to his obsession. Turning back to Long he said gently, "Long Qi, would you do me a great favor? I believe you and your family to be people of stability and virtue. My Ming emperor is dead. He gave me this vase as a gift of honor, but now it brings me only sorrow. I would like you and your descendants to be its custodians. Cherish it as a symbol of a greatness that has passed, and keep it in your family as long as it is humanly possible. Your family may have need of such a treasure in the future."

Long turned ashen, his face quivering, "No, impossible," he whispered. "It is too valuable. What would people think?" His agitation became so great that Wu reached his hand out to calm him.

"No one need know," said Wu. "It will be our secret and the secret treasure of your family to come. I will write a letter to accompany it explaining that I gave it to you as an unencumbered gift. I shall put my seal to the letter. It can be kept with the vase. My future is uncertain. The paths of a general are perilous. The vase will be better in your safe-keeping. It will not help me win battles. It might even be destroyed in the process. Why should such a beautiful thing cease to be?

Go now and fetch me something to eat. The sky is already pale, and my advance scouts tell me that Li-Zicheng is not many *lis* distant. It promises to be a full day. I will need my strength. When you return, I will have the letter and the vase prepared for you."

Long opened his mouth to protest again, but Wu raised his hand in a gesture of silence. "Go. I have decided."

Long Qi left in a daze— elated — humble — fearful and somehow greatly changed. He carried the vase as though it might burn his hands.

Returning to the present, Jing Lingzi looked at her son and said, "That is Long Qi's story of how we gained our legacy."

"What an incredible tale!" Long Qiong shivered then looked intently at his mother. "Is that why ... but what has become of the vase?"

"Come," she pulled him along toward his father's grave. "You will soon see it." Then, unwrapping a trowel from the blue shirting material, she knelt down on the moss at the north side of the grave mound and began to dig.

"Ah, yes, here." Out of the earth she extracted an object encrusted with layers and layers of cloth and dirt which fell away under her careful unwrapping. Several oiled cloths covered the inmost bundle which held a metal box. Nested inside it was a smaller, beautifully decorated box no more than 16 centimeters long. Jing Lingzi removed the box with reverence and opened it. They both stared, mesmerized by the exquisite object lying on its bed of red silk. The wind played on the sweat generated from their movements causing Qiong to tremble with a frisson of excitement while the cold sweep from the past touched him with an ineffable sadness. The present seemed so trammeled, so unsure. He looked at his mother and spoke.

"This is actually ours?" He couldn't grasp the reality of what he had heard and what he was seeing.

"Yes, yes ours," murmured his mother. "It will take some time for you to get used to the idea. I know."

"And this, what is this?" asked Qiong as he touched a small bamboo tube which lay under carefully crafted retaining loops in a depression in the silk to one side of the vase.

27

His mother's hand closed over his. "Don't open it," she said quickly. "It contains the letter which Wu Sangui wrote to accompany the vase. Through the years it has become very fragile. Some time ago, one of our ancestors decided that his descendants should memorize the contents of the letter so that there would be no need to handle it, but it must always be kept with the vase. It is proof that it belongs to us."

"Our past," said Qiong softly — "my connection to the man in the portrait."

They both continued to gaze at the vase in thoughtful meditation. Then suddenly shaking herself, Jing Lingzi looked nervously over her shoulder even though they had passed no one for the last half hour of their journey. She slowly closed the box and painstakingly wrapped it in the shirting material. She put the bundle carefully inside the food basket and then began, with Qiong's help, to replace the dirt in the hole and tamp the moss back as it had been. Finally, they both said a brief prayer at the grave mound. Gathering up the basket which held their treasure, Jing Lingzi looked at her son. "Your father must be happy now, Qiong. I have done my duty to our ancestors. You are the next generation; now it is up to you."

She turned away from him with resolve. "Tomorrow I will go to stay with Auntie Xu and find a good place for our legacy to rest during these difficult times. I'll let you know when it is safe and where it is. This is to be yours and your child's also. You know you are not so young," she cajoled. "You must marry soon and have a child before I am too old to be an interfering grandmother." She chuckled then and reached for his hand. Holding the basket between them, they walked back to the village to take the train home.

Qiong found little sleep that night. His brain felt like watered rice — his mother leaving for who knew how long — the noise of another night of hooligans roaming the streets like wild dogs with Mao's blessing, and the worry over the safety of the vase —all these things made him wonder if he would ever sleep again.

"Surely," he thought, "Wenshi will not demean himself by handling the cooking pots behind which the vase is hidden. And certainly no thief would ever suspect us of having anything worth stealing. How many sleepless nights have my ancestors had guarding this *thing* down through the years? Ah, but such a beautiful thing, an object worthy of the Son of Heaven — and our link to our past."

Finally, Qiong fell into a troubled sleep. His dream was frighteningly real. He was struggling to pull a wide cloth of blue shirting material behind him as he waded through the deep snow at the edge of a forest. In the center of this makeshift sled his mother sat, upright, cradling the box which held the Ming vase. Even though she weighed very little, the effort of pulling her seemed incredible. He was sweating from exertion and fear. And always, at the edge of his vision, behind the first screen of evergreens in the woods, the tiger kept pace with him. It was all he could do not to break and run.

Chapter 3

Jilin, China

April 28, 1990

Rachel Toussant shook her head in disbelief. Sometimes the unreality of it was overwhelming. Here she was a fifty-four year old divorced woman teaching English in Jilin, China. Last year she had not even been aware that Jilin existed. When she was a child and she and her father, a geography teacher, had poured over the maps of exotic places with lovely sounding names, Jilin had been called Kirin and the area was called Manchuria. She had liked that name, Manchuria — Manchuria. Its exotic sound had made her determined that someday she would explore it herself. It was both more and different than she could have ever imagined. The year was nearing its end. Manchuria was now a part of her psyche in a way she could never have predicted. In his frequent letters, her fiance, Phil Barrett, jokingly told her that this phenomenon had occurred because she had been Chinese in a past reincarnation. The fact that he taught religions of the world in the same college where she taught, might tend to lend some weight to this theory even though she knew he was gently teasing her.

She had not had time to be really lonely, but she missed Phil terribly and was constantly grateful for the circumstances which had brought him into her life. When the chance had come for her to go to China, he said, "Go for it. I'll be here when you get back." And she never for a moment doubted that he would be.

Anytime she felt deprived of human touch, Rachel took a bus ride. Unless it was an off time of day, she was guaranteed tactile contact of the most pressing sort. Most Chinese buses were jammed with passengers packed in so tightly that, going around a corner, the passengers swayed in concert like sheaves of wheat in a windy field. One of her friends had actually had the buttons ripped from her coat during the in-out stampede at a bus stop. Even at the modest height of five feet, five inches, Rachel was taller than many of the people on the bus; thus she could at least breathe.

Today was congestion at its worst because of the spring festival at Beishan Park. Her *waiban*, Long Qiong, who was in charge of the foreign teachers at her university, had warned Rachel not to come. "Too many people—too dangerous."

As far as she had experienced, however, the only real danger to a foreigner working in China was from pickpockets or in getting lost. The Chinese people were generally so helpful that they wouldn't permit you to be lost alone. In their eagerness to help, they often compounded the problem mightily. Different people gave totally contradictory directions with an air of conviction that they alone knew where a foreigner might want to go and how to get there. Often as not they were wrong.

Pausing to catch her breath after the bus spewed its passengers out, Rachel looked with fascination at Beishan. From where she stood, the mountainside seemed to undulate with a constant ribbon of small figures proceeding up and down the wide cement pathway between the two mountains. At the top, the mountains were connected by a spanning bridge called *Luanpei Bridge* on which dozens of people milled about looking down to the cement path far below, or out to the vista of the city in the distance, or to the other mountains surrounding those supporting the bridge.

Rachel loved this place. She had been here many times during the past year with her friends and also with some of her students. She had even organized a field trip here for her graduate students who, surprisingly, knew almost nothing about Buddhism and the temples on Beishan. She had been afraid the university officials would object to the trip, but after she had convinced the head of the graduate studies that it would result in good essay opportunities for her students, it was listed as *social investigation* and had proceeded without a hitch.

She could remember the day of the student trip well. The aged Buddhist nun with the benevolent face had spoken in Chinese to her students about the history of the temple. The nun had retained her calmness even when discussing the destruction of parts of the

32

temple during the Cultural Revolution. She spoke quietly about the nuns and monks being assigned to either factories or the countryside to work "to further the glory of the People's Revolution." But later in the talk, the nun's face had contorted with hatred as words shot out of her mouth like spit sunflower seeds. Startled, Rachel had leaned over to a student in the back and asked him to translate.

"She says when the Japanese came they were pigs. Many bad things happened. They should all die horrible deaths."

So much for the Buddhist all-encompassing compassion Rachel had thought, but the students seemed completely undisturbed by the contradiction.

When they left the temple that day, she and her students had started across *Luanpei Bridge.* The students stopped midway to lean over the waist-high railing, watching with great interest as the insect-like figures far below progressed up the cement path which passed under the bridge. After the path wound underneath the bridge, it gradually rose up the side of a third mountain in the back where it split into several paths, two of which doubled back to connect the mountains on either side of the bridge and came to a stop at both ends of the bridge.

"What is the name of the bridge?" Rachel had asked.

Someone said, *"Luanpei."* The students looked at each other knowingly. There was a long pause. Then Zhao Rong, one of the most vocal spoke, "Sometimes it is called *'Broken Back Bridge.'"*

"What a strange name. Why is it called that?"

Again the long silence. "Perhaps ... perhaps because during the Cultural Revolution people were unhappy. Some people thought this was a good place to die."

"Here?" Rachel could feel all her students assessing her face.

"Yes, so far down—the cement is so hard. Surely the back would be broken," Zhao said with a neutral passivity. Again a long pause and the assessing looks, then her students began chattering all at once moving on in a clump to sample the offerings of the *ice cream* vendor who served what amounted to sugar-flavored water on a stick.

Now, Rachel watched the tiny figures streaming back and forth across the bridge and wondered how many of them had dark memories of this place.

Today she was to meet a number of her friends, also Americans who were working in Jilin. The friendships they had formed were the strong kind that foreigners often experienced as a small community in a strange land. Even though most of the teachers were much younger than she, Rachel felt easy with them and younger herself when she was with them. They had become very precious to her. Unfortunately for her, but perhaps fortunately for them, she had become a sort of mother confessor to them even though she certainly hadn't applied for the job. It made things difficult because she liked them all. She didn't want to know that Melanie had worked in Sidney Mance's gallery as an apprentice while she was in art school in San Francisco. She didn't want to know about her affair with Sidney, especially when Laura Mance, Sidney's wife, was also one of Rachel's friends. But she was glad to be able to help Melanie deal with the pain she felt. She was reminded of the sociograms of a fourth-grade class she had been required to plot for one of her education courses her senior year in college. *John likes Mary, but Mary likes Al etc.* At least fourth-graders weren't in the habit of falling in love with the wrong people. She wasn't sure she wanted to meet Sidney Mance. His advance press was none too good. There was still a little time to explore the festival before meeting her friends, so she set off toward the temple complex. Inside the temples, Buddhist and Daoist figures were mixed in what seemed, at least to a foreigner, to be a complete porridge of religion. It was rather like entering a Western church to find a plaque in honor of Martin Luther on one side of the altar and a weeping Virgin Mary and holy water on the other.

Before the festival, it had been no use trying to get a clear explanation from the students at the university as to what to expect. They had matured under the *religion of Mao* and understood none of what was resurfacing among their elders or the people of the countryside. Theologically speaking, her students were truly a *lost generation.*

This particular festival had drawn over twenty thousand people to Beishan park. Rachel was amazed by it all. Hundreds of small, doll-like figures were arranged around the feet of almost all of the statues. Sakyamuni Buddha had the largest congregation of dolls, but the guardians of the North, the South, the East and the West also had their share. Even the most remote figures had plentiful doll audiences awaiting some kind of transcendent event which would validate their existence. Incongruously, money in the form of *mao, jiao*, and *yuan* notes was stuffed between the toes and fingers and even in the ears of most of the statues giving them a rather jaunty, frivolous air. China had always been a land where bribery worked wonders. Presumably, it even worked with the gods.

One of the older Chinese teachers at the university had told Rachel beforehand that she was quite sure that the dolls represented children who were ill, and that each doll had been made by the parents to look like their child. Supposedly, at the end of the festival, the dolls were burned and the bad *qi* which possessed the children was destroyed in the fire.

Although she longed to use her camera, Rachel knew that it would be impolite to take photos. After all, this very public festival concerned very private pain.

She looked up the mountain and could see a clot of people on the steps leading to the highest temple. In the center of that group, high above the other heads, the red hair of Melanie Hazen gleamed. Next to her the curly black hair of Paul Solomon contrasted with the straight hair of the Chinese, who, always curious about the strange behavior of foreigners, clustered around the whole group. Laura Mance was there with their Chinese colleague, Frank Li. Frank had served as Laura's interpreter for the past term and possibly, Rachel feared, had served as more than just that. The pretty man in the impeccably pressed suit (how did one achieve that in China?) must be Laura's husband, Sidney Mance, the man much discussed and anguished over by Melanie Hazen. Rachel squared her shoulders and proceeded. "This should be interesting," she mumbled to herself. Two other people, Chinese surely, but with the air and dress of foreigners, also stood with her friends. Perhaps they had come with Sidney Mance.

As she approached the group, Rachel noticed that Melanie was talking and gesturing with much more than her ordinary exuberance. Her bracelets clanged and her voice rose in what seemed like a frantic agitation that she couldn't seem to control. Paul Solomon watched her sullenly; Laura Mance was pale and subdued; Frank Li watched Laura with a protective stillness that had a tinge of danger to it. Sidney was in discussion with the two strangers.

Rachel observed the strangers carefully before they noticed her. The woman was close to fifty. She was not pretty but had strong competent looking features. Her beautifully cut grey suit and her simple but expensive black bag and flats proclaimed her to be a fairly sophisticated woman. Her splendid black hair was fashioned in the kind of geometric cut only to be obtained at some large city outside of China. The man was a little harder to read—an extrovert to be sure. He was wearing what would be called a reporter's or safari jacket in the pricier American catalogs. It was a garment of many pockets designed to permit the wearer to carry every conceivable need from maps to pocket knives. This wearer had obviously taken the ads to heart because maps, pens, tape measures and other paraphernalia protruded from every pocket. Rachel was later to see him pull a rather large paperback English/Chinese dictionary from one of the two copious side pockets. The opposite pocket with its intriguingly heavy sag held a wicked looking device that turned out to be an innocent acupressure wheel with two stainless steel balls covered with spikes. The contraption was connected by a handle and could be rolled over arms, chest thighs, or even the back of the neck. Even though the man looked Chinese, he, also, seemed to be a *foreigner.*

Laura glanced up and saw Rachel approaching. She detached herself from the group and ran over to Rachel, grasped her hand and pulled her along saying, "I'm so glad you're here. Come and meet Sidney and his colleagues." Rachel walked over thrusting her hand out for a warm *glad to meet a fellow American* handshake only to find it firmly clamped between Sidney's two hands much in the way an undertaker would press the hand of a bereaved client to indicate deep sincerity. She looked him in the eyes and completely understood the problems she had been hearing about. As she pulled her hand back to keep it safe from further assault, she reflected wryly that there were advantages in being at an age where the hormones gently nudged rather than dictated. She certainly missed Phil's straight-forward charm.

Sidney Mance was a man who practiced his charisma almost unconsciously to keep it finely honed much as an athlete might absentmindedly stretch and bend to stay limber. She glanced at Laura and saw misery sitting firmly on her shoulder. Frank looked none too joyous either. Melanie looked frantically angry. Paul was distressed, but Sidney seemed to be oblivious to the undertones swirling around him. He was in the best of moods. He gestured expansively toward his two companions. "This is Claire Lucas," he said indicating the sophisticated Chinese woman. "She works for me in my art gallery in San Francisco. She's quite knowledgeable about oriental art. She and her mother worked for my father before his death. When I took over his gallery, I was naturally anxious to keep Claire with us."

Rachel noticed the pursed lips and firming of Claire's jaw as Sidney spoke, but Claire swiftly extended her hand to Rachel and gave her a radiant smile.

"I like her," Rachel thought, "But I wonder what that was all about?" Rachel grasped her hand and said, "I'm very glad to meet you, but I'm surprised to hear such an American name."

Claire laughed. "Well, my name is actually Zhao Jie. I was born in China in 1941. During the Japanese occupation after father was killed, my mother fled to Qingdao to live with my grandparents. She met an American officer there. He and my mother were married. He adopted me, thus the name, Lucas. In 1948, he took us to the United States with him and I've lived there ever since. This is the first time I've been back to China. I'm afraid I don't remember much although I do have pictures in my head of Qingdao."

Sidney interrupted her to add, "Nevertheless, she jumped at the chance to come here. Didn't you Claire?" The smile he bestowed upon her was less than convincing. Claire smiled back. Her eyes levelly meeting his did not match her mouth.

"And here," Sidney motioned toward the man, "is a fellow American business man. Meet George Kim."

Again Rachel sensed some sort of tension belying the hearty introduction.

Kim bounded to her side with an outstretched hand.

"Mr. Kim." Rachel grasped his hand. "And what kind of business are you in?"

"It is a complicated business, I'm afraid. I come to China to buy silks. Then I send them to my Uncle's textile plant in Seoul where they are made into evening jackets for the American market. My Uncle ships them to me in Carmel where I distribute them to various boutiques in San Francisco and Los Angeles. It is quite profitable, plus I get to travel a lot."

"So then you're not Chinese but Korean?" Rachel asked.

"I'm a Chinese-Korean by birth but an American by choice. My mother was originally from Jilin. She studied in Yanji near the Korean border. She met my father, who was Korean, there in Yanji. He fought in the Korean war and survived only to die shortly afterwards in some kind of military accident. After his death, my mother returned to Jilin. I even attended the Yuwen Middle School here for a while."

"You mean the same middle school that Kim Il Sung went to?" questioned Rachel. "Are you by any chance related to him?"

George Kim laughed, "Only in my mother's wildest dreams. I must confess that I enjoy knowing that there is a statue of a Kim on the school grounds. Have you seen it?"

At that point a chorus of, "Of course." came from the others. Melanie added, "That's one of the first points of interest that we were trotted around to—the middle school of the illustrious Korean leader. We also saw the hydro-electric dam where Li Peng worked before he really worked himself into something more damning."

Everyone laughed at her joke and then began discussing the festival and the trip to the Changbai Mountains scheduled for the following week.

"While we're there, I'd like to step over the border into North Korean," declared Paul, "just to say I've been there."

Melanie snorted, "You sound like the African student from Changchun who wanted to go to Vladivostok because we are so close."

Paul shot her an irritated look. He was obviously the unrequited lover when it came to Melanie, and it did not improve his temper for her to respond to him in such an offhand way.

Frank Li spoke up, "I don't believe that is possible for Americans. They are still *personae non gratae* to the North Koreans."

Melanie giggled, "Laura's even teaching you Latin now I see."

Frank looked at Laura apologetically and then quickly looked at his shoes as if regretting having drawn attention to himself. Rachel could have shaken Melanie. Such cattiness was unlike her. To relieve the tension she turned to George Kim and asked, "Perhaps you can tell us a little about what happened here in Jilin during the Cultural Revolution."

Sidney interrupted, "I've been hearing stories that some of the fool Chinese who couldn't take it did themselves in at the bridge we just passed."

George looked directly at Sidney and spoke with careful precision, "That is true. My mother was one of those 'fool Chinese.'" He spun around abruptly and walked off in a crunch of gravel. Claire Lucas hurried after him. Sidney just shrugged and rolled his eyes.

"Oh, Lord!" thought Rachel. "Why did I have to ask about the Cultural Revolution?"

Melanie and Paul, also embarrassed by the exchange, suddenly spotted a vendor in the distance with wares that they had to see. Rachel decided that it was a good moment to detach herself from the group with promises to meet soon for dinner.

"I think I've inadvertently stirred the pot," she said to herself with much chagrin.

Chapter 4

When Rachel had gone, Laura and Frank stood with Sidney in an uneasy silence. Laura finally spoke, "Sidney, how could you have said that? Didn't you know anything about his background. I thought he was a friend."

Sidney had the grace to look uncomfortable, but he replied, "Oh, George is ... George is more of an employee than a friend. I really don't know him very well. He's always been such a glad-hander. I didn't know he had a sensitive bone in his body. He's actually working for me, you know, as a picker. He has good contacts here in China and he speaks the language. He's in a great position to find good antiques for the gallery—and he has. George has a good eye. I'm sorry, but I'm sure he'll get over it. Look, its too marvelous a day to waste worrying about George. Let's look around."

As they wandered around the festival, Sidney reflected that it was, in fact a fine day, bright, crisp and scented with all manner of exotic smells. George had already found him some superb antiques, and he, himself, had set in motion the plan by which he would acquire the antique to surpass all antiques. Too bad that Laura was so withdrawn. She had a pinched, pasty look and seemed extremely preoccupied. She surely couldn't know about his relationship with Melanie. No, of course not. Melanie would certainly not be about to tell her that. Maybe his idea of having them both spend a year teaching here in China had been a bad thing. His position as head of *Teachers for a New World* did mesh nicely with his gallery. He could make tax exempt trips to China to visit the teachers he had placed and pick up a few choice objects in the bargain. Not a bad setup.

They passed a number of vendors hawking things ranging from candied crab apples to religious medals. Something caught his eye, and he leaned over to Laura and said, "Darling, would you ask Frank to go back to that last vendor on the left and get the large Mao button in the center of the blanket for me?" He had started a little collection of Cultural Revolution memorabilia that the Chinese were getting rid of now that Mao was no longer revered as he

41

had been. Frank was very adept at getting the lowest price on anything. In the short time that Sidney had known Frank, he had found him to be quite useful.

Seeing Sidney here, out of the context where he was always in charge, gave Laura a changed perspective on his character. She thought, "I never realized before how typical Sidney's lordly behavior is. He knows that Frank's English is good, yet he didn't speak directly to him. I actually believe that he regards the Chinese in the same way the English colonials did. How stupid." Laura turned to Frank speaking rapidly in Chinese. He immediately returned to bargain with the vendor. When Americans started looking at anything, the price automatically quadrupled or more.

Sidney was annoyed when Laura and Frank started talking in Chinese, but it didn't occur to him to even question his own lack of communication with Frank in English. All he knew was that these unintelligible exchanges felt threatening to him in some way. Still, that had been one of the reasons he had placed Laura here as a teacher—so that she could learn the language well enough to be useful on his buying trips for the gallery. He could tell that she had achieved a much better command of the language than Melanie had in the same amount of time.

Frank returned with the pin handing it to Laura who in turn gave it to Sidney. Laura looked at Sidney tentatively, "Sidney, let's go back. I'm getting awfully tired. I just don't feel like any more today."

He put his arm around her, squeezed her shoulders, and in a cajolingly earnest voice said, "But, Darling, this is so enjoyable. It's important to have you with me. The air will do you good. You look like you need more exercise."

In truth, she was afraid she would vomit at any moment. The whiffs of greasy food from the passing vendors and the crush of chattering people were just too much. She remembered her mother telling her about how sick she had been when she was pregnant, but Laura could never have imagined this constant nausea almost as though the baby were trying to escape from her mouth. She knew her untenable position added to the sickness. Shortly after she arrived in China she had discovered that she wasn't Sidney's only *Darling*, but she hadn't intended any kind of revenge. Frank just happened. And now, in an amazingly short time, she loved Frank in such a sound, complete way that she knew beyond any doubt it was right. There was no possibility of staying with Sidney any longer. Trying to deceive him was repugnant to her. Even if she had been willing to try, she could hardly claim the baby was his. She hadn't been with him for months. Anyway, the child certainly would not look very Caucasian.

In China, the solution was easy — abortion. But to her and to Frank that was unthinkable. It was *their* child conceived of their love. Every night she racked her mind for a way out. She could not imagine living the rest of her life here, but she would not live it without Frank. If she and Frank could marry, she could take him to the States with her. She was certain, though, that Sidney would never consent to divorce. His pride was too great. Despite his protestations of *universal love* he was a tough cookie when crossed. Why hadn't she recognized that when she first met him? Those soulful blue eyes did it to almost everyone. He could fix you in his gaze and say the most outrageous things and make them seem like gospel. It was impossible! What a mess she had made of things. There had to be a solution.

Chapter 5

Long Qiong was once again taking a train ride of great importance. His brother had been right those years ago when he had warned Long Qiong to hone his farming skills. Shortly after their mother had gone to Yanji, the universities were closed. Qiong had been sent to the countryside as a laborer. The joke was that he had been a good peasant. As a child, he had worked hard and knew the ways of the farm. Ironically, his formal schooling had not been wasted. His knowledge was a constant companion enabling him to carry on long dialogues in his mind while he performed his monotonous duties.

His clever brother had not fared as well. Some misstep, or perhaps just natural political changes, had soon seen him also planting rice in the countryside, an elite Red Guard transformed into a disgruntled peasant with no companionable inner resources.

Still, the whole family had survived better than most through those awful years. Now, both he and his brother worked in the university in Jilin. Long Qiong was *waiban* in charge of foreign guests and teachers there. His brother worked in the business office where his natural cleverness was utilized to its fullest. Long Qiong's wife, dear Chan Lumei, also worked at the university, but she had been ill since that terrible time last June and spent as many days in bed now as at the school. There was nothing the authorities could do. She was ill from a sickness of spirit.

Their only son, Long Fu, had left the university for Beijing last April full of high purpose and the idealistic enthusiasm only the young can have. Long Qiong and his wife watched the unfolding of the events at Tiananmen square with hopeful pride coupled with a pressing sense of foreboding. On June 3, their worst nightmares became reality. Long Fu disappeared in the *turmoil*. In the days that followed, Chan Lumei alternated between a manic activity beseeching local officials for news and a total depression during which she barely acknowledged her own existence. She was incapable of concentrating on anything but her misery. He, himself, spent every spare moment following leads gathered from bits of information which he gleaned from more fortunate students who were at Tiananmen and had returned. He had traveled to Beijing twice. When he was there, he realized that his connections were so pitifully small that he had little hope of finding his son or even finding out what had happened to him.

It was ironic that, only recently, when China seemed to have a brighter future, disaster had stricken him personally. For weeks he had felt impotent. Then, slowly, he formed a plan of action. The very corruption the students had protested against could be his ally. Large amounts of money produced miraculous results. He now had a way to get that money.

Last year, his university had hosted a Chinese-Korean, a George Kim, who lived in America. He remembered clearly the evening Kim had talked to him in private after one of their banquets. Kim had run after him as the group was leaving and clapped his hand on Qiong's shoulder saying, "Long Qiong, there is something I've been wanting to ask you. You've lived here for quite a number of years, haven't you."

Qiong indicated that he had.

"This is somewhat delicate but you seem like a discrete fellow. I ... a ... well, in addition to my business with my uncle, I've also been finding Chinese antiques for the American market. Americans pay very well for these things, and I thought you might be in a position to hear about anyone who might need to sell something. Anyway, I'll give you my card. Keep your eyes open will you?"

At the time, what Kim had said didn't seem to have any relevance for Qiong, but for some reason, he had kept Kim's business card. When Long Qiong's son, Long Fu, disappeared during the Tiananmen turmoil, Long Qiong thought of Kim. By the time Kim came through the province again in September of 1989, Long Qiong had a pressing need for money. He approached Kim with his plan. The decision to sell the family's Ming vase had not come easily to Qiong, but he reasoned that its purpose was to benefit his family. This was an emergency of the highest order. What could be more important than saving his son who was the youngest member of the Long clan? He had only to persuade his mother. Long Fu was her only grandson. It must be done.

He had no illusions that he would get a fair price from Kim. But if he got enough to find his son, that would be a fair price indeed. Kim said that he would immediately contact the man for whom he worked, Sidney Mance, with a description of the vase.

About three weeks later, Long Qiong received a letter written in impeccable Mandarin. Mr. Mance was indeed interested in the vase. Mance requested that Qiong deal with no one but himself directly, and especially not with Mr. Kim. Mance also requested that Long Qiong use his influence to place Mance's wife, Laura, as a teacher of English at the university for the spring semester. Qiong was not to mention the vase to her, but could deal directly with him since he was planning a trip to China in April.

Long Qiong was in a quandary. He could not send a letter with specifics about the sale of the vase to Sidney Mance without the possibility of someone reading the contents before it left China. But Mance had asked that no further dealings should be made with Kim. It seemed his only option was to grant Mance's request concerning his wife and wait until spring even though every day without news of his son was agony. Fortunately, Laura Mance had good credentials, so it was easy to grant the somewhat unusual request for a teacher to be placed for one term only. In the ensuing, necessarily guarded correspondence with Mance, he learned that the man was not only the owner of a gallery in San Francisco dealing in oriental art, but also the director of a foundation called, *Teachers for a New World*. He had been placing teachers in China for several years. Two of the teachers, Melanie Hazen and Paul Solomon, who were on the train now with the group traveling to Yanji, had been placed by Mance to teach at one of the hospitals in Jilin.

Mance had appeared in China in April approaching Qiong through Mance's secretary, Claire Lucas who spoke Chinese well. It was she who had corresponded with him in Mandarin.

The trip to Yanji was an excuse to pick up the vase from his aunt's home without anyone knowing about it, not even Mance. As *waiban* of the university, Long was expected to plan trips to entertain the foreign teachers. Other local schools often welcomed the chance to send their teachers along and share the cost; thus, the hospital and a chemical company, which had several Japanese teachers, plus a university in Changchun were sharing the costs of the train car.

The visit to Yanji was a success. The Americans were suitably impressed by the beauty of the Changbai Mountains, and they thanked Qiong sincerely for making the trip possible. He had arranged for several vans to take the group beyond the timberline to the glacial, Heavenly Pool, which was actually more the size of a lake. The weather had cooperated. In the clear air, the sun shone brilliantly on the absolute stillness of the turquoise water so that the lake looked like a jewel set among the prongs of the mountains surrounding it. It sparked at the command of heaven in a setting seemingly outside of time. All of them felt this and spoke in hushed tones trying to imprint this picture on their minds. Later, they had hiked down the mountainside to the tree line where they were met again by the vans.

The Changchun group of teachers, which was composed of two fundamentalist Christian couples, Sissy and Stephen Turner and John and Marcie Morrison, had been told by someone that the mountains were home to an especially poisonous species of snake. Stephen sidled up to the two Japanese teachers, Hitomi Monamura and Chieko Isu and said in a concerned tone, "Do watch where you walk. We know for a fact that there are very poisonous snakes in this area."

The two Japanese teachers did not speak English well, but they understood *snakes* and *poison*. They responded with gasps and widened eyes which seemed to be very gratifying to Stephen. This news, however, didn't seem to faze the rest of the group other than making them a little more vigilant about where they stepped, but Hitomi and Chieko were terrified. They walked along the surface of the path as though it were strewn with hot coals and bordered with demons who wafted through the trees mysteriously on the shafts of light and the pine scented breeze. Rachel was irritated with Stephen. It seemed to her that he had set out to deliberately spoil things.

Qiong, who was very sensitive to his surroundings, understood the two women's unease. It may have been his anxiety about the purpose of the trip, but something was making him respond to every shift of wind and the creak of the pine boughs as they rubbed together. Who knew? Perhaps in such a setting demons did exist.

From the mountains, they traveled to Fangchan, the spot where China, North Korea and the Soviet Union meet. They had picnicked on a high plateau which overlooked the area. The Americans had prepared the food which they had, somehow, made to taste different from the food Qiong was used to. One of the couples from Changchun had made bread that seemed very strange, not at all like the soft pasty Chinese bread. Between two pieces of this bread they had put more pork than he would have used for his family's whole meal. Rachel had handed him one and said, "Qiong, try something typically American. We call it a sandwich."

Qiong had lifted the bread tentatively to see what was inside. Then watching what the others did, he held it in both hands and took a large bite out of it. He had to admit that he enjoyed it. Even the yellow paste which was spread on top of the meat was quite palatable.

Long Qiong had planned for the group to spend its last day visiting the area of the Tumen Gate near the North Korean border. For some reason, the Americans found the idea of such close proximity to *enemy* territory exciting. Qiong knew that the trip would take a full day; consequently, he arranged for the *waiban* from the chemical institute to be in charge. That way, he was free to visit his mother.

The Tumen River area was very commercialized near the gates. Many vendors of the kind usually found around Chinese historical sites vied for business from the group as soon as they alighted from their vans. In what was already a beautiful setting, the vendors had felt it necessary to gild the lily by setting up cardboard mountains to which artificial flowers were pinned in garish clusters. Cardboard deer and tigers romped side by side while the god of longevity, Shou Lao, rested serenely in his two-dimensional splendor under a false pagoda.

Paul was the first to comment with a groan of disbelief, "My God, I can't believe it — a poor man's Chinese Disneyland."

"With a touch of high church—" Melanie added, bowing low to the cardboard Shou Lao.

The Turners and the Morrisons just frowned in distaste at the cardboard god, but they made no comment. Claire Lucas said in a soft puzzled voice, "But the scenery here is so beautiful without ... all this."

Rachel, who had long since decided that the aesthetics of the old and of the new China had not evolved in an unbroken line of continuity, remained undisturbed by the decorative enhancements. Perhaps the Cultural Revolution was to blame for the new aesthetics; but whatever the cause, the effect was incongruous.

As the women walked along the wall bordering the river, they were besieged by various entrepreneurs who urged them to don a traditional Korean costume and have their pictures taken in front of one of the splendid displays.

"Ladies," one of the vendors implored. "Be making your person beautiful in a Korean dress."

At first everyone resisted, but the fantastically designed and colored costumes which hung from stalls waved enticingly in the breeze. Rachel finally succumbed. "I don't know about the rest of you, but I can't resist this unparalleled opportunity to be making myself beautiful," she declared. She began looking through the costumes for the perfect one. Immediately, the other women in the party entered into the zaniness of her mood. Finding costumes to fit all the women was a challenge. Melanie was especially funny. None of the Korean gowns was long enough. Consequently, she presented an absurd picture with her sturdy hiking boots showing underneath an elegant red and yellow silk gown with voluminous sleeves. She had the nearby vendors convulsed with laughter as she did a pseudo oriental dance clanking her bracelets in rhythm to her steps while her clunky boots extended out gracefully in great strides back and forth. Paul entered into the mood by approaching Melanie and saying, "My honorable lady, you must buy some of my bearpaw salve to rid you of your freckles and make your beauty complete."

"Peasant, the ground deer antler and the ginseng you have consumed have made you bold beyond your station," Melanie retorted tossing her head. Even Laura, who was uneasy around Melanie, couldn't help giggling. Frank Li stood nearby with a wistful look on his face. He seemed to want to enter into the joking but didn't know how.

Sidney looked exasperated. He gave Laura a sharp look of displeasure, but for once, it had no effect. She, too, was caught up in the lightness of the day and totally ignored him. Sissy and Marcie plunged into the selection as though shopping were their true vocations, while Hitomi and Chieko tried to communicate with the vendors in their limited Korean.

Rachel had a different problem with her costume from the one which Melanie had. The yoked bodice opened at a slant over one shoulder; the long skirt was gathered above the bust line and flowed in an unfitted sweep to the ground. Theoretically, the style should have been a *one size fits all*; however, there was a slight problem in the bust area. It became obvious that oriental women tended to be smaller there than many American women were. One of the women vendors finally solved the problem.

"Easy to fix," the vendor said confidently and handed Rachel a fan to hold. Then she raised Rachel's hand so that the fan covered the spot where the costume gapped.

"There, so see, it is working," the vendor proclaimed as she beamed at everyone. Then the woman, encouraged now by a cluster of other vendors who held their hands to their mouths to hide their giggles, arranged the group picture.

Melanie was the centerpiece. She stood behind a bench on which the vendor seated Rachel so that the skirt of Rachel's dress completely hid Melanie's boots. With much pushing and leading, the other members of the group were placed in the tableau. Laura and Claire, who sat on one side of Rachel, and Hitomi and Chieko, who sat on the other side, looked most authentic. Their costumes fit and showed off the delicate grace that the original Korean wearers would have had. Marcie and Sissy stood behind the bench on either side of Melanie like two bouffant-haired bookends. Melanie's red hair made a central halo with a life of its own. The resulting picture was a triumph of nonsense which pleased all the participants. George Kim ran around arranging the cardboard tigers and deer in poses of admiration centered on the group. "Ladies, look this way," he shouted. "Now, ladies, a more serene expression if you please. Ah, perfect."

Paul wanted a picture of Melanie alone. "Melanie," he suggested, "Surely, you can"t leave this country without a picture of you and this fine fellow over here." He was motioning to the larger-than-life size Shou Lao.

"But I know nothing about him," she objected with mock concern.

Frank Li brightened visibly at her words. At last he could be a part of what was going on. He cleared his throat, "I believe," he said, "that Shou Lao would be a very auspicious personage to take a picture with. He is the god of longevity. He fixes the times of a person's death, but he can change his mind if he is persuaded strongly enough. He is a stellar deity. one of the ... ah ... seventy-five bureaucrats under the jurisdiction of the Great Emperor of the Eastern Peak."

"Such nonsense," snorted John Morrison. The others from Changchun nodded in agreement.

Frank looked abashed. "Of course, this is just an ancient legend," he said. "No one, or very few people, believe it nowadays."

Paul added, "Crazy, even the gods have a bureaucracy in China. It figures."

Melanie felt sorry for the discomfort the response to Frank's remarks had caused him. She quickly moved to stand beside the figure of Shou Lao and said, "I'm ready for my picture now. It is an honor to stand next to one of such renown."

The men in the group watched, adding ridiculous comments. Rachel found it interesting to see that the Chinese *waibans* would only permit themselves to enjoy the moment after they had first observed the behavior of the American men. She thought that it must be awful to have to live with such control that few things could be spontaneous.

To the echoes of *piaoliang, piaoliang* (pretty) from the vendors who also thought the foreigners' money was pretty, the women paid for their photos content to have a bargain unlike any other bargain they had purchased.

The whole group walked to the edge of the river and looked across to the opposite bank. North Korea began in the middle of the river where a sign in English, Chinese and Korean was placed which read: *People in boats are forbidden to hand goods to people in boats nearby. It is forbidden to move from one boat to the other absolutely.*

"I'm sure that the North Koreans put that sign there because so many English speaking people are dying to live in North Korea." Paul said sarcastically. "Absolutely!"

George Kim smiled slowly, "You are probably right in your skepticism; however, I would bet that many items have been handed back and forth over the invisible border in the middle of the river." He gave Sidney a wink, but Sidney chose to ignore it. He turned to Laura and snapped, "Now that you've quit playing the tourist, perhaps we can go on to the Tumen Gate." Rachel had the feeling that it was only politeness which kept the rest of the group from hissing at Sidney.

The Tumen Gate was an imposing modern structure of concrete block topped with an overhanging orange lintel. It was decorated with plaques of vigorous looking Chinese people laboring happily, presumably for the sake of the republic. More traditional symbols of China, guardian lions, stood in front of each side of the gate.

Beyond it, a beautifully paved wide road which was lined with ornate light posts wound surrealistically toward the distant green hills of North Korea. The hills were totally untouched by signs of human habitation. The group fell silent. All of them were following their own thoughts down that winding road.

Chapter 6

While the foreign teachers and their guests were visiting the Tumen Gate, Long Qiong was traveling north from Yanji, anxious to speak with his mother and persuade her to give him the Ming vase. He got a ride into the countryside from a farmer whose friendliness helped to dissipate the tension Qiong felt at the coming reunion. His aunt's ginseng farm lay in a flat valley. Behind the fields of ginseng with its red berry toppings, dense forests spread out to the base of the nearby mountains. The house was made of a kind of stucco, low to the ground with a heavy thatched roof. The small windows prevented heat loss in the bitter winters of the area. A fireplace built against the outside of the house served for cooking in the summer. A similar fireplace inside was used for cooking in the winter and, it also heated a *kang* by shunting the hot air of the fire through a large pipe which ran under the raised bed platform inside the house. Quilts and blankets were piled on top of the platform to trap the heat radiating from it. It made a cozy bed. He saw that, in addition to the main well, a second well and water pump had been added to the half enclosed cooking-food preparation area. Surely, Auntie Xu had become prosperous. A number of outbuildings had also been built since he had last been here. The farm even boasted a small greenhouse, probably for experimenting with improved strains of ginseng.

As he approached the house, he could see his mother and his aunt hurrying down the path. Within minutes, he was clasped in his mother's arms while his aunt stood behind him stroking his head and murmuring as she had when he was a little boy. Qiong had not realized how lonely he had been. His son had vanished; his wife had turned into a walking ghost; the contact of family now made him realize what the terrible year had done to him.

The faint smell of onions and garlic on his mother's skin brought back memories of a time when he had felt safe. He was close to tears.

The women pulled him into the house. Then they began to rush around trying to outdo each other in their offerings of food for

55

his approval. His mother had cooked delicate strips of chicken dipped in egg white and then fried quickly in hot oil. Never, he thought, had he tasted anything so delicious. His aunt had made *baozi*, large dumplings with a pork and vegetable filling. There were caramelized walnuts, eggs fried in tomatoes and vinegar, pork in sweet soy sauce and, of course, ginseng tea.

"Qiong," they had both said throughout the meal. "Eat more. We will think you do not like our cooking."

Ginseng roots which were suspended in jars of water lined the shelves looking like tiny, withered men dancing in an amber sea. His mother had decorated the walls with pictures from old calendars he had sent her. On the beds, white cotton over covers protected the incredible silk covered quilts which, with Chinese practicality, revealed their splendor teasingly through a small hole cut into the center of the top. He could have stayed there forever.

He didn't know how to broach the subject of the purpose for his trip. The enormity of what he was asking made him mute. Thus, he was amazed when his mother began pulling a trunk away from the wall. She extracted a package from a hiding hole behind the trunk and offered it to him.

"You will want this I think." she said handing it to him.

He opened it without speaking. It was the Ming vase he had seen so many years ago.

"How did you know I would ask for this?" Qiong asked. "How could you know?"

"Hush," she said. "Do you think I am a stupid woman? Auntie Xu and I have discussed this over and over. It is the only way to get enough money to find Long Fu. After all, it is merely a vase. Long Fu is family; he is my only grandson."

Long Qiong found himself arguing the opposite point of view even though it was he who had come to ask for the vase.

"But the vase is what has made our family special down through the years."

"Bah," said his mother. "Has it ever made the birth of a child easier? Has it ever kept death away when it was time? We can be special without a vase. Long Fu is special. Why should we save the vase? If he is not found, there will be no family. Wenshi is getting older and set in his ways. I do not think he will marry now. The vase must be used for our family. It is right to do this."

"And what if we give it up, and Long Fu is still not found?" asked Qiong.

"Then we will have done everything we could." his mother countered. "There is no other way. The matter is settled."

"Now tell me," she asked, "Is Chan Lumei any better?"

It was then that Qiong began to cry, slow, silent tears which he had held in so long by a superhuman will.

"You would not know her. She is like someone who has no ears — no eyes; yet she looks at terrible scenes in the distance which no one else can see. I don't know what to do."

His mother embraced him, rocking him back and forth in her arms. "You will find a way to do what you must." she whispered.

They talked until it was time for him to leave. Qiong rose, reluctant to go. His mother looked as though she wanted to say something else but couldn't make up her mind to do so.

"I'm so stupid," thought Long Qiong. "I'm not her only son." He turned to her and smiled. "You will be happy to know that Wenshi has just received a promotion in his office at the university. He is doing well."

It was what she had wanted. She beamed back at him. "Thank you, my son, for remembering to tell me that when you have so much on your mind. You are a good son. Now I know you must go. May good fortune go with you."

He could feel the two women watching him walk down the path until he was almost out of sight. When he turned, they seemed like two small children waving wildly in order to be seen. He was sure that smiles were fixed on their faces, but he also knew that their eyes would be as wet as his were.

Chapter 7

Now back on the train for the return journey, Long Qiong felt drained, yet he knew he had to marshal the resources to get through the next few weeks. Sidney Mance had balked at waiting until after the trip to see the vase. Long Qiong feared that Mance suspected that the reason for the trip was to retrieve the vase from somewhere near Yanji. This thought made Qiong incredibly uneasy. He felt so vulnerable with something of such immeasurable value in his possession.

Seated across the aisle from Long Qiong in the train compartment, Rachel surveyed the passing scenery. On the way to Yanji, she had been surprised to notice that the landscapes near the end of their journey had reminded her of the Sawtooth Mountains in Idaho. The wheat fields, which were plentiful in this part of China, contrasted sharply with the emerald rice fields of the South. They also gave Rachel the impression of belonging to a stretch of the United States. She realized how good it would be to return home.

The train passed villages of Koreans who had settled in China. True to her impressions gained by talking with the Chinese, the Korean settlements were immaculate. "Very clean, very clean," the Chinese would say shaking their heads in wonder as though being so clean required some kind of minor miracle.

Rachel hadn't expected the tunnels that they had passed into on the way down. Going through them had been a bit disconcerting because, with the usual frugality of the Chinese who even turned their bus headlights off for night driving, the train was plunged into total darkness as it charged ahead.

Now, returning to Jilin, she felt comfortably familiar with the rhythms of the train and luxuriated in the soothing motion as it rocked along. It would be night by the time they arrived, plenty of time to relax and enjoy the changing scenes which passed outside the window. When she thought of the Chinese passengers in the hard seat section, she felt a little guilty having all this soft sleeper space with its separate compartments. Still, it was a ten-hour journey; the privacy was welcome. This was something that would not have ever occurred to her just a year ago. She hated the crush of the crowds, but reflected that it was really quite remarkable, given the sheer numbers of people, that things were as orderly as they were.

Her year here was hardly enough time. She knew she would come back to China some day. There was so much she did not understand— so much to learn. She found that many of the Chinese she had met possessed a subtlety of mind inconceivable to most Americans—probably more a result of their history rather than anything genetic, she thought. Just to survive the Cultural Revolution had required both a subtlety and an endurance of the highest order. She had tried to keep all this in mind in her dealings with Qiong, but the man was still a mystery to her.

They often disagreed on what she could or could not do. He treated her as though she were made of eggshells, but she supposed since he was responsible for her, and because she was older than most foreign teachers, he tended to consign her to a different category. She knew that most Chinese women retired at fifty-five and were then content to take care of their grandchildren and engage in the activities of the older citizen. She had been amused at a sign she had seen near the Ming Tombs north of Beijing outside a toilet. The usual signs for men and women were written in both Chinese and English; however, in addition, this sign designated one of the toilets as being for the *oldy and the weaky*. She definitely did not feel as though she was there yet.

She had learned bits and pieces from her students about most of the people at the university, so it wasn't long until she was able to put together the story of what had happened to Qiong's son. It was amazing that he could carry on with his work under the circumstances. She felt great sympathy toward him and wished her Chinese were good enough to let him know how much she admired his hard work when every hour must bring him such hellish speculations. In her mind, not knowing was the worst sort of torture. She supposed that Qiong and his wife had not even been able to follow the events of Tiananmen on their television as she and Phil had been able to do in America before she left.

When the countryside flattened out for a stretch and the scenery became much the same, Rachel turned to her book of selected Tang and Song poems with pleasurable anticipation. One of her Chinese teaching colleagues had given it to her. It was a remarkable anthology with the original poems on the left-hand page in Chinese characters under which was the pinyin Romanization in Chinese sounds. On the right-hand page, depending on the amount of room, were two or three English translations of the poems by various eminent nineteenth and twentieth century British and American poets. She well knew the difficulty of faithfully translating poetry from one language to another. Often it was an outright impossibility. What was intriguing, was the variety in meaning which the different translators had imposed on these Chinese classics. Oh, how she wished she knew Chinese well!

The Li Bai classic which all Chinese school children learned was one she had learned also and often recited to herself as she thought of Phil. She liked the translation by Arthur Cooper best:

> Before my bed
> there is bright moonlight
> so that it seems
> like frost on the ground.
> Lifting my head,
> I watch the bright moon.
> Lowering my head,
> I dream that I'm home.

Despite her absorption in the poems, Rachel could not help being aware of Qiong's agitation. He seemed even worse on this return trip than he had been going to Yanji. She looked up and ventured a smile at him. He nodded his head slightly and smiled back, but his eyes darted nervously around—from the compartment door to his small duffle bag beside him, to the window, then back to the door again.

Why was he so jumpy—almost frightened with a strange kind of excitement that wouldn't let him rest? She decided it would be best to seem to be still absorbed in her book. A few seconds later, having finished reading a poem by Wang Wei, she glanced up and was startled to find a handsome Chinese man staring intently into their compartment through the glass in the door. She made an involuntary noise of astonishment at which Long Qiong jerked his head around to glare at the intruder as the man pivoted abruptly and disappeared. Qiong threw himself at the door, opened it, and lunged into the aisle in time to see what he though was a familiar back disappear through the car's connecting platform to a door which swung closed on the next car. "Could it be Wenshi?" he asked himself. "Surely, he can't know about the vase!" But he felt an added burden of fear at this possibility. Wenshi had, to be sure, calmed down as he matured, but he was still unpredictable. Qiong did a little two-step of indecision forward and then back toward his duffle bag, seemingly drawn into two different directions by opposing impulses. Finally, he made up his mind and sat down again beside the bag as though none of the previous frantic activity had occurred.

Rachel suddenly felt claustrophobic with all the random energy Long Qiong was exuding into the compartment. She turned to him and said, "I think I'll go to the dining car now. Would you like to join me?"

Qiong shook his head slowly, "No, I'm not very hungry, but perhaps a bowl of rice ...?"

"Certainly, I'll be glad to—and tea?"

"No, I have some here. The attendants will bring the hot water around soon."

"All right, I'll see you in a little while," she replied.

She hurried out of the compartment feeling guilty about the relief she felt in getting away from Long. As she moved toward the dining car at the front of the train, she looked into the compartments between her's and the next car. The very next compartment was occupied by the Mances and Frank Li; however, only Sidney Mance seemed to be in the compartment. Beyond that compartment was the compartment of George Kim and Claire Lucas. Melanie Hazen and Paul Solomon, who seemed to be engaged in a low-key argument, were in the following compartment. The one beyond theirs was empty. The toilet or *cesuo* was the final compartment in their car. The platform connected to the next car, a hard sleeper in which Chinese passengers were crammed six to a compartment. Even this was not as bad as the hard seat car further on where the passengers sat on benches with no divisions. The hard seat cars were fascinating in their activity but difficult to travel in for long. The noise and the smoke (most Chinese men were addicted to cigarettes) and the hardness of the benches made for uncomfortable travel. Rachel had enjoyed several two-hour trips in this kind of car, but that was about all she could stand.

As she made her way through the cars, she drew the attention of the Chinese passengers. They seemed to be fascinated by the foreigners (*waiguorens*) and studied them as though to memorize the kind of clothing they wore, the style of their hair, and the sounds of their voices. Rachel had even had strangers on a bus ask her if her teeth were real. Many people in China initiated a kind of naive intimacy, even with strangers, that she found delightful.

After her meal, she would visit with some of the rest of her group. She was very fond of Laura and Frank, so she supposed she could bear Sidney for a short time. George Kim and Claire Lucas were both connected with Sidney's gallery. She would like to get to know them better. She was also interested in Chinese art. Laura had said that George was looking for antiques for Sidney's gallery. She had just met Sidney, but she couldn't imagine how Claire could have endured working for him for so long.

A group of Japanese teachers occupied the compartment on the other side of hers, and beyond that were two American couples, the kind of religious people that Paul Solomon would disparagingly call fantastic fundamentalist freaks. They kept pretty much to themselves as far as mixing with other foreigners was concerned; however, throughout the year, Rachel had often seen them engaged in intense conversations with prospective Chinese converts. Her Chinese students thought these Americans were very strange and asked if many American women had long painted nails, bouffant hairdos, and what she would call Tammy Faye makeup. Rachel assured her students that America was a land of diversity. All American women *did not* look like that. She did have to give those women credit for being able to maintain such perfection despite lack of water and other conveniences in China which Americans took for granted in their own country.

A group of high ranking Chinese military men noisily conversed in the next to the last compartment at the far end. The train attendants' room, where water was heated for the tea which all train passengers drank, was the final compartment in their car.

Chapter 8

As Rachel entered the dining car, she placed her book of poems on a small table near the door, and settling herself in the seat, tried to determine what she could safely eat. She knew that the tea and the rice would be all right, and she could live on that. She looked at the soupy vegetable mix on the table next to hers.

"Suspicious looking," she muttered to herself, "probably full of *wei jing*" (better known in America as MSG and shunned by all who were prone to migraine headaches.) The Chinese were mystified that this, to them, essential ingredient gave many Americans a colossal pain. Well, she would be safe. She had some fruit with her and the delicious jellied red bean bars. Rice and tea it was. After all, it was doing marvels for her figure. Having ordered, she sat back and turned her attention to the others in the car. Laura Mance and Frank Li were seated several tables away to her right engaged in a subdued conversation totally unaware of anyone else. Laura's thick auburn hair emphasized the paleness of her face. Her fine features were drawn. Her green eyes, which normally shone with enthusiasm, lacked lustre. Frank's face, usually animated by his intelligent expression which was enhanced by the rather 1950's horned rim glasses, looked grim.

Rachel did not intend to eavesdrop, but during a lull in the conversation of the other passengers, she clearly heard Laura say, "... *women haizi* ..."

Things suddenly clicked into place. "*Women haizi*—our child." Of course! The delicate bluish look of Laura's eyelid (and she never wore makeup) was exactly the same as Rachel's daughter's had been during the first months of her pregnancy. And Laura had complained of the *flu* several times recently. The implications took Rachel's breath away. It couldn't be Sidney's child. She wasn't showing, and she had been here in China for five months. What a disaster! If it were Frank's, the Chinese were not as casual about such matters as Americans had become in the past few years. Rachel liked both of these young people very much. Concern for them made her forget about eating.

Her thoughts were interrupted by a "Pardon Madam." Looking up, she saw a very tall Chinese man with a warm sensitive face hovering over her table.

He continued, "I am Lu Xing the *cheng jing* ... ah ... what you might call the train detective. Would you do me the great favor of talking some English with me? I'm, ah, learning myself."

"Teaching myself," Rachel said automatically. "Oh, how rude!" she thought, "to correct his first sentence. I must get out of my teacher mode."

"Just so, Madam, thank you. I am teaching myself. How do you think of the weather?"

Such a delightful man, but she must control the amused twitch at the corner of her mouth. After all, her Chinese was abysmal.

"It is lovely here in the Northeast," she replied. "It reminds me of my home."

"Ah, very good. Perhaps from time to time we will speak. Now I must not disturb you more. Thank you, Madam."

"My name is Rachel Toussant. You may call me Rachel," she said as she offered him her hand.

He took her hand and squeezed vigorously. "Yes, yes, Rachel ... it is the American way to be familiar."

Rachel smiled at him. "Only with people we like," she replied.

"Then I hope you will be liking me." He glanced at her book. "I too read poetry. Li Bai is a favorite of all Chinese. And Miss Dickinson—the American — I like. Now I go. But I will return. See you bye and bye." And with that, he hurried out of the car.

With her spirits somewhat lifted, Rachel finished her meal. Laura and Frank were still in the dining car when she left to return to her compartment. As she approached the platform in front of her car, she saw George Kim and Claire Lucas. Claire stood looking out the window with her arms folded across her chest. The scene appeared to be one of intimacy which had just been broken by some sort of disagreement. "At least they're aware I'm here," Rachel thought. She wasn't sure she could assimilate any more startling revelations. Suddenly everything went absolutely black.

"Oh, I'd forgotten the tunnels," she said aloud. Claire gave a nervous giggle. George continued to smoke uninterrupted by the blackout. Rachel could see the tip of his cigarette glowing. They stood still, waiting for what seemed a very long time until the train re-emerged into daylight. While they were in the tunnel, Rachel saw the beam of a flashlight moving ahead in her car, but it was impossible to tell just where it was.   As soon as the train cleared the tunnel, she left George and Claire standing there and made her way to her compartment.

In the compartment, Long Qiong lay sprawled on the floor, arms and legs splayed out against the seats at impossible angles. For a moment Rachel just stared, then she called out, "Please someone, help!" People began pouring rapidly into the narrow aisle causing a mass of confusion. The Americans could understand her, but she had completely lost any ability to communicate in Chinese. In a few seconds, her new friend, Lu Xing the train detective, was pushing his way through the crowd around the compartment door. At about the same time Long Qiong groaned and propped himself up on an elbow and then promptly vomited. "Oh, Lord," thought Rachel, "well at least he's alive." Lu Xing called out orders rapidly in Chinese to one of the train attendants. The mess was soon mopped up and Lu Xing had Qiong half lying, half seated in the compartment. During the next few minutes, Rachel's mind processed the scenes around her like a set of rapidly changing slides projected one after another. She saw Long Qiong raise himself up with a look of absolute panic only to fall back with a pathetic groan. George Kim was standing to her right looking very thoughtful. Claire Lucas was behind George looking back and forth between him and Long Qiong with a puzzled expression on her face. Sidney Mance, who stood in the doorway of his compartment, was holding a bottle of beer and nonchalantly eating an apple. Laura and Frank Li had moved up the aisle, presumably returning from the dining car, to stand huddled together in the aisle near the doorway of their compartment. Laura had a container of rice in her hands. Paul Solomon was craning his head out of his compartment, and Melanie Hazen stood in the aisle with the Japanese teachers outside of their compartment. The members of the religious contingent were jabbering among themselves with hushed shock, while the military men barked orders to the train attendants demanding to know what had happened. They were, by and large, ignored.

Lu Xing looked up at Rachel. "Please," he said, "some medical aid." For a moment she looked blank. Then she went to the attendants' room, grabbed up a first aid kit she saw lying there and returned to the compartment. By that time, Lu had ordered all of the onlookers to return to their compartments until he was free to ask them questions. With the help of one of the attendants, they bathed the sizable lump on Long Qiong's head with an antiseptic and gave him some tea. They could do nothing for his spirits. He looked as though someone had died. He answered Lu's questions in apathetic monosyllables. "No, I cannot imagine why I was struck. No, no ... nothing is missing. Please, I am all right. It is nothing." But he said this with such a tone of despair that both Lu Xing and Rachel looked at each other in consternation. They were baffled and frustrated. Lu drew Rachel into the aisle.

"He is more colorful now," Lu said. "He should be all right, but you must observe him. OK? I will ask others what they know."

It was true. Long Qiong's color had returned; however, Rachel knew head injuries could be tricky. Qiong roused himself long enough to look quickly into his duffle bag. Then with an awful sigh, he tossed it aside and lay back with his eyes closed. Rachel seated herself in the compartment and continued to read from her book of Chinese poems occasionally glancing across the compartment to check on Long. His breathing became slow and steady. "Good," she thought, "sleep is probably the best thing for him." She had forgotten the rice he had asked for, but, at this point, sleep was better for him than food she reasoned.

Soon Rachel became less interested in the poems and more interested in a trip to the toilet.

"Surely" she argued with herself, "he'll be all right for the short time I'll be gone." She gave him one final look, tiptoed out of the compartment, and hurried down the aisle to the *cesuo*. Fortunately, it was not occupied.

Long Qiong had been aware of Rachel leaning over him. Through half closed eyelids, he saw her quietly leave the compartment.

"Good," he said to himself, "now I can think. I must decide what to do." His head ached horribly, but he had to sort things out. Should he tell the train detective about the vase? What if that had been his brother outside the compartment peering in? If Wenshi knew about the vase, surely he would understand why Long Qiong needed it so desperately now. He couldn't have stolen it, could he? His brother wasn't *that* bad. But if Qiong explained about the vase and told that it had been stolen, then others would know, and it might be even harder to recover it.

It was suddenly dark again—another tunnel—his body tensed. He was ready this time.

Chapter 9

Sidney couldn't believe his good fortune. When Long Qiong had said, "You can't see the vase until after the Yanji trip." Sidney knew almost certainly that Qiong must be going to Yanji to get it. He watched Qiong closely as they got on the train for the return trip. His guess was right. He was taking inordinately good care of his old duffle bag—one that he had practically ignored on the trip there. Sidney had wandered up and down the aisles as often as he could, casually looking into Qiong's compartment as he went by. He racked his brain for a way to successfully remove the vase from the compartment. After all, why pay for the vase if he could just take it? He was sure that the Long family had kept their possession of it an absolute secret. If it happened to be stolen now, Qiong would probably remain quiet in the hopes of somehow recovering it.

What occurred next was, without a doubt, fortuitous serendipity. Laura and Frank decided they were hungry and wanted to go to the dining car. Sidney pretended to be absorbed in the latest issue of *Arts of Asia* and had begged off, asking them to bring something back for him.

When he saw Rachel go by, his heart started pounding and his brain had gone into overdrive. Long Qiong must be alone! What now? Subconsciously he remembered the tunnels they had passed through on the way down. If fortune smiled upon him ... if Laura and Frank and Rachel stayed away long enough... if... He looked around rapidly. Yes, he had a small flashlight. Frank's bottle of beer and several apples lay on the table by the window. The bottle should do nicely for a little tap on the head. Vulgar, certainly, but practical. The blow couldn't be too hard, or he'd be in deep trouble. It was certainly worth a try.

It had worked beautifully. The Ming vase was his now! He had been greatly relieved when Long Qiong regained consciousness. He had no intentions of being a murderer. The hubbub in the aisle was dying down, but he was so elated that his mind was racing noisily. Laura and Frank were, once again, seated in the compartment. Just before they came back, Sidney had hastily placed the box with the vase in it onto the upper bunk under his pillow. He didn't expect a search, but it was too vulnerable there. He must get them out of here again.

Laura was looking at him rather quizzically. Her look concentrated on the bottle of beer in his hand. Sidney had been afraid it would foam all over after the vigorous tap it had administered to Qiong's head, but again luck held. He was able to quickly and neatly flip the top off and had been casually drinking from it when Qiong was discovered on the floor of his compartment.

Finally, Laura spoke raising her eyebrows in a question, "But Sidney, you don't like beer?"

"No, you're right. Frank, I'm sorry to have pilfered yours, but I needed something to wash down a couple of pills with — had an awful headache — hope that was OK." Sidney smiled at Frank.

Frank didn't smile back. Sidney rarely spoke directly to him. This was a change. He nodded his assent without saying anything.

"As a matter of fact," continued Sidney, "the pills didn't help; the beer only made it worse. If you could ...?"

Leaving the sentence unfinished, he gave them his most winsome smile.

Laura's face regained some of its usual animation. "Of course, I'll go talk to someone in one of the other compartments and let you rest." She turned to Frank. "I'm sure you can find something to do for a while."

He nodded and hurriedly left, walking toward the empty compartment next to the toilet. Laura followed him there.

Sidney was relieved to finally be alone again. There was definitely something wrong with Laura. She had always been quiet, but now she darted brief, disquieting glances at him almost as though she were afraid of him — strange. But he didn't dwell long on those speculations.

He could feel the vase above him burning its presence through the box as though it were sitting under an x-ray machine. He longed to place it on the table underneath the window to examine it in detail, but that would be the height of folly. Instead, he moved it and the pillow down to the lower bunk and placed it in the corner between himself and the window. Then he got several large bags down and emptied some of the contents onto the little table that jutted out underneath the window. He could pretend to examine his other treasures while stealing an occasional brief look at the vase beside him.

If he re-packed with the vase hidden inside one of the larger bags of antiques, it should be protected until he got to Jilin. Fortunately, the vase was small.

He ranged the finds from the Yanji trip in front of him — a pair of *paktong* candlesticks with an intricate pattern of encircling dragons and cloud forms should bring at least $3,000.00. Not bad considering that he paid a street vendor $80.00 U.S. for them. He needed to find out more about *paktong*. The Chinese called it the magic metal with the soul of gold. He knew it was a combination of copper, zinc and nickel. This combination produced a silvery object which could be highly polished but was harder than silver and did not tarnish. The design of the candlesticks was exquisite — about twelve inches high, square in shape with a gently flared top and an even more greatly flared and weighted base — an excellent find.

He held up an 18th century Korean bronze vase. It was a beauty! The bronze, which had turned black from age and oxidation, was covered with a finely wrought inlaid silver design of willow trees and scrolls that spread around the bulbous body and up into an attenuated neck which was about five inches long. If the silver were carefully polished, not disturbing the bronze, it would be stunning. Sidney pulled out two Koryo dynasty spoons with swallow tail handles, also from Korea, and a textile rank badge with a painstakingly embroidered phoenix amid clouds and waves.

He checked the door to the aisle, then stole a brief look at the Ming vase beside him. It was enough to make a person weep — its beauty and its age ... ah.

He would have to rely on George to get most of the antiques out of the country without papers. George was good at that. He usually took a ship from Dalian to Korea and must have established great connections (*guanshi*) because he never had any trouble with customs. On his return to the U.S., he generally came in through Mexico, again seemingly with little problem.

Getting the Ming vase out would present a greater risk. He wasn't sharing this with anyone. It had to be a do-it-yourself project. He planned to fly to Guangzhou and then take the train to Hong Kong. He was confident that a sizable amount of *foreign exchange currency* would make the transfer easy. It might not even be necessary if the customs people didn't check his bags carefully. He broke out in a cold sweat just thinking about the possibility of having the vase confiscated. A similar piece had sold at Christie's last year for $230,321.00, an amount he remembered to the dollar. He had a private client for this one. The client had limitless resources and an obscene addiction to Chinese porcelains. Sidney was sure he could name his price.

He wondered idly whether George Kim had believed him when he had explained that the vase Long Qiong was talking about had turned out to be a clever fake. Well, it didn't matter. There was absolutely nothing Kim could do about it.

Everything suddenly went black again. Another tunnel. But why should he be nervous? Nevertheless, he clutched the box containing the Ming vase in an instinctive grasp. With his other hand he groped for his flashlight. A shaft of wind from the opening door made the window curtains flap. A beam of light swept over the table picking out the candlesticks, then the Korean vase. Abruptly the light shifted, hitting him full in the face. The bronze vase scraped as it was snatched from the tabletop. Sidney was paralyzed by fear.

Blinking, he knew a moment of absolute terror as he flung one hand upward to protect himself. The other hand grasped his prize even more tightly. Then both hands fell and were still. The bronze vase was tossed out the window. With another flap of the curtains, the compartment door closed again.

Chapter 10

Rachel had just reached for the door handle to leave the toilet when everything went black again. "Oh, bother, another tunnel!" She had to get back to Long Qiong. She grabbed the handle, scraping her knuckles against a sharp piece of metal on the door jamb.

"Damn," she yelled and plummeted out the door into another person who let out an "uhf" of breath.

"Madam, madam, calm yourself. It is I, Lu Xing. I recognize your angry noise. The sun will soon shine in the train."

Hearing his voice, she immediately felt better and stood still for a few more minutes until his prediction came true. The light was blinding after the complete darkness of the tunnel.

As she and Lu Xing stood blinking to adjust to the sudden light, she saw Laura Mance backing slowly toward them emitting low moaning sounds. Laura turned and looked at them both with wide, unseeing eyes. She pressed her knuckles to her mouth, then suddenly sagged against the outside windows of the aisle. Bleating soft little "oh's," she pointed her arm toward her compartment. Rachel caught her in her arms as Lu Xing rushed past them and slid the door of the Mance compartment open.

Sidney Mance lay slumped over the small window table. A narrow trickle of blood seeped under a candlestick poised on the edge of the table and ran over the edge to form a small pool on the floor. Mance's right hand was extended above his head across the table as though reaching for support from the rim of the table. The mate to the candlestick and several other objects lay scattered on the floor. An apple had rolled into the far corner. Two pillows were tossed carelessly into the corner opposite Mance.

Lu Xing carefully stepped over the objects on the floor so as not to disturb them. He gently turned Mance's head. A blow to the left temporal bone had crushed the skull. Small bits of brain tissue extruded from the damaged area. Lu was surprised that there was not more blood. Sidney Mance was, indeed, dead.

Lu Xing had seen death many times. Suicide and violence were everyday events during the most awful days of the Cultural

Revolution. During that time, China had writhed in an orgy of insanity. Peoples' spirits had become twisted. Neighbor did violence to neighbor, sons and daughters did violence to parents, friends could not rely on friends — all this madness had occurred in the name of *devotion to correcting errors of thought*. Recently, things had seemed to be better until the spasm of terror last year at Tiananmen. But here on *his* train, which he always though of as a friendly oasis transporting people back and forth in the excitement that journeys brought, violence shocked him. It made him exceedingly angry. He was responsible. He must do something.

Lu noticed a camera on the upper bunk. He pulled it down, trying not to disturb anything else in the process. He turned to see Rachel behind him in the doorway. He backed out of the compartment and handed the camera to her saying, "Please, Madam, take some pictures for me. It will help us remember how things are."

She looked at him doubtfully. "Must I?"

"Please," he replied. "It will be helping me much. I'm not sure on working the American camera."

Rachel felt a strong repugnance for her task. She completed it quickly, advancing the film out of the camera with hands gone suddenly clumsy and then turned to go look after Laura whom she had left lying in the empty compartment. Lu pulled lightly at her arm.

"Madam, I must ask for your kind help."

"Why me?" Rachel asked. She though irreverently, "I wonder why Chinese men call me madam. I must break him of that habit."

"Because I must talk with all the foreigners. Your English is so ... fluent," Lu said.

Rachel looked at him as though he were demented. "Well, I have been practicing it for fifty odd years," she said. The sarcasm was completely lost on Lu who was totally preoccupied in thought. He nodded absently, "Most true. In addition, I heard you in the bathing room making angry noises when the time of the murder must be. In consequence, I know you could not do it. I also do not believe Long Qiong is the culprit. He could not murder well with a sore head."

Rachel had forgotten about Long Qiong's injury. She looked hastily into her compartment only to see Long Qiong apparently asleep as he had been when she left. She couldn't help smiling at Lu's *Chinglish*. Sorehead, indeed.

"You're probably right. He got quite a knock on the head. Do you think the same person ... ?"

Lu shrugged his shoulders.

Rachel said, "All right. I'll help, but Laura needs someone with her."

By then a crowd had again gathered in the aisle. Rachel turned to Claire Lucas who was standing with George Kim in the doorway of their compartment and said, "Claire, Could you stay with Laura for a while? She shouldn't be left alone at a time like this. She's resting in the empty compartment next to the toilet."

Claire nodded, gave George an undecipherable look, and went to take care of Laura. When she entered the compartment, Frank Li was sitting beside Laura holding her hand and watching her still face with anguished concern. Laura's eyes were closed and she was breathing shallowly. Claire sat down on the other seat feeling like an intruder and said apologetically, "I was asked to help Laura. Is there anything I can do?"

Frank gave Claire an annoyed look. "She just needs quiet," he retorted. Claire glanced at Frank's hand which was holding Laura's. When he saw her staring, he felt a tremendous sense of guilt, but he would not let go. He had to laugh at himself as he remembered one of the first personal things Laura had said to him. "Chairman Mao has made you into a nation of Puritans," she had said. When he had asked her to explain what she meant, she had told him that the Puritans were among the first settlers of America. "They were idealistic and had very rigid moral codes. Unfortunately, they had as many human frailties as others. Consequently, they often couldn't live up to their codes, but they always suffered massive pangs of guilt when they didn't."

Frank looked again at Claire trying to appraise her as though she might be able to answer some of his doubts. He longed to ask her if it was very difficult to be a Chinese in America, but of course that question was absurd. She *was* an American. She had lived there most of her life. For him it would be different ... if they survived this. He was determined he would not lose Laura. He

77

reflected that many Chinese people had been put in jail for less serious offenses than those he and Laura had committed. Some were even jailed for what they thought, or, for that matter, what someone who disliked them thought they thought.

When Laura had come into his life, it was like someone had thrown wide the shutters on a window letting light and air into a room which had been dark and musty. A clean perspective had renewed him and swept away his vague fears. He hadn't even realized he was afraid, but he supposed the apprehension he felt was endemic among the people of his country.

Because his English was excellent, the English department had asked him to help the new foreign teachers, so he tried to arrange trips which they would find interesting or supply things they requested. He specifically remembered an exchange he and Laura had one day when she wanted to do something (he couldn't even remember now what) but he had answered with his usual, "Perhaps." She had compressed her lips and looking him levelly in the eyes said, "Say yes or no. Don't always equivocate. What are you afraid of?"

The comment caught him by surprise. What was he afraid of? Nothing—everything. Since the Cultural Revolution, few individuals dared to make instant decisions. They weighed all the possible consequences, sought the confirmation of their colleagues and bosses, and, in general, tried to foist the decision onto someone else just in case it was the wrong one and they would be blamed. He began to admire this woman who wasn't afraid. It hadn't taken long for that admiration to turn into a genuine love. After that, nothing could ever be the same. He sighed deeply. Claire looked at him sympathetically. "She probably does understand," he thought. "For her, also, things cannot be made simple. One can never unlearn new ideas, new feelings."

After Claire had gone to sit with Laura, Lu Xing set about restoring order to the bedlam in the car. He raised his voice, shouting above the buzz of questions and speculations. "I must demand you to return to your compartments. A man is dead. I will explain to all. In turn, I wish you to tell me all you know."

Immediately, the voices became silent. Lu continued in a lower voice, "I am asking this kind lady to help me." He gestured to Rachel. "Mance is murdered ... dead. You must help to find the killer. Please be thinking. We will be speaking with each one of you."

The occupants of the car remained in the aisles staring at him. He gave an exasperated wave of his arm saying, "Now go, sit. I will come." He repeated his words in Chinese for the benefit of the military group and the attendants.

When the onlookers were gone, he turned to Rachel and asked, "Can you see anything gone."

Rachel shook her head glumly. "No, I barely knew him, but it certainly doesn't look like robbery — even I can recognize the value of those," she said as she pointed to the antiques lying on the floor. "Perhaps Laura ... but she's really not able to now."

"No, no, it is natural not," agreed Lu. "Will you secure the compartment? I must find the attendants. If it was a thief who did this, I wonder why so many beautiful things were left."

Having heard Lu's command of "go sit," the attendants had done just that, returning to their room at the end of the car to whisper with hissing excitement. Lu Xing ordered them to accompany him to the Mance compartment to help and also to observe his movements. In China, one rarely did anything official without witnesses. It was the Chinese way, the safe way.

When the compartment had been searched, Lu said, "We will lay down Mance's body in here, and the compartment will be safe with the attendants sitting on the jump seat in the aisle outside at all times." Lu explained this meticulously to the attendants. "No one must enter the compartment other than myself or this lady," he said.

Having given his instructions, Lu stepped gingerly inside and retrieved the antiques which were scattered on the floor. He placed them carefully into the empty bag which was beside the body. He put it and another full bag of antiques on the bunk above. He looked at the window; it was open. He would have expected it to be in this fine weather. Then he turned his attention to the pillows, picking each up carefully and examining it. There was a small blotch of what must be blood on one of them. The bleeding from the wound had not been copious, but just maybe some trace of blood might have gotten on the killer. He could barely hope for such luck though. The pillow must have been in the corner to the left of Mance between him and the window in order to be bloody at all. Lu handed the pillow carefully to one of the attendants instructing her to put it in a plastic bag and lock it in the attendants' compartment. Finally, Lu moved the luggage belonging to Frank Li and Laura Mance along with the bags of antiques nearer to the door. These were also to be sent to the train attendants' room.

Lu gave Rachel an appraising look and said, "We will now move the body."

"We?" said Rachel weakly. She noticed that the two attendants had distanced themselves as though guessing what Lu's next request might be; even though neither of them probably understood enough English to know what he had said to Rachel. Lu eventually became aware that his potential helpers were shrinking from the task. He spoke rapidly to the attendants in Chinese. They stood mutely shaking their heads back and forth slowly. He compressed his lips in anger.

Rachel wasn't sure whether the attendants were opposed to handling a dead person in general or just reluctant to touch dead foreigners, but opposed they were. Lu's anger didn't budge them. He looked again at Rachel and said more moderately, " Sometimes my countrymen are like children. It must be done. Soon he will be like a stick."

Rachel frowned, "A stick?" she said. Lu closed his eyes and stood rigidly at attention in a pantomime of death.

"Oh, I see, *rigor mortis* — it is called *rigor mortis*."

"Ah, *rigor mortis*—like a stick. This I will remember," said Lu seriously as he filed it away in his mind for some future contingency.

Rachel nodded her assent. She would help. She hoped she wouldn't do something stupid like vomiting or fainting, both of which seemed highly likely.

"We will put him on this seat," Lu said, "head to the window. You move the feet."

Rachel did as instructed wondering what Phil would say if he could see her now ... not in his wildest dreams!

The body which had housed Sidney Mance was now stretched out onto the seat with a blanket from the compartment lying under him. One of the attendants, having regained her courage, handed Lu another blanket. He took it absently in his left hand while he stared at the body. He was memorizing the position of the wound, but he was doing much more. Once again in his life he was meeting and trying to understand death. A few moments ago this body had possessed emotions, sight, sense of smell, breath. Where did all that go? He hated the opaqueness of death. Perhaps if he believed in something it would be easier. But what? He said softly, "The Daoists say *death is the opposite of time.* Do you know the meaning of this?"

Rachel didn't try to answer. She knew Lu was talking to himself. After a moment, he pulled himself up taller, lifted Mance's head gently putting the clean pillow underneath it, and turned it so that the wound did not show. He spread the blanket carefully over the body. Then he reached for Mance's unopened luggage and set it on the floor. He sat opposite the body and beckoned to Rachel to sit beside him. "We must look at his things with sharp eyes," he said briskly. "You can tell me about Mance *Xiansheng* as we look."

Rachel was decidedly not pleased to be remaining there, but she knew it was necessary for the moment. "I just met him, but I had heard about him from both Laura Mance and also from Melanie Hazen. Melanie's the tall young woman with the red hair."

"The one who is very much angry and makes the noise with her bracelets?"

"Well, yes," replied Rachel thinking over his impression, "perhaps you could say angry — excitable certainly. Anyway, from the little I know— knew, about Mance, I came to the conclusion that he was a very murderable sort."

"Pardon, Madam, I do not understand."

"Oh, I'm not even sure that murderable is a word. What I mean is that he was not an honest man with other people. I suspect he may have been just as dishonest in the business of acquiring art works for his gallery as he was in his personal relations. I sense that there may be many people he has harmed."

"Ah, I see," Lu Xing murmured, "Perhaps his wife?"

"Yes," answered Rachel reluctantly, "perhaps his wife." A very uncomfortable feeling was taking its hold on her. "Look," she said, "These are my friends. They are good people. I really can't do this." She didn't suppose Lu would know the word *stool pigeon*. She wished she knew the Chinese equivalent.

He gave her an earnest and understanding look. "Possibly this is all the murdering, but possibly there is more. I will try to take care of these friends of your. One who murders can not be a friend. The Daoists say *A murder is a stone thrown in a pool. The water moves and can't be stopped.* Please, Madam, We must find a murderer in a few hours before the train comes to Jilin. You must tell me what you think and what you know. It will be best for most, truly."

Rachel knew he was right. "I may not have any friends when this is over," she thought to herself. "But we can't leave things this way."

Chapter 11

Lu clapped his hand to his head in consternation. "There is too much to think of," he said. "I must talk to the attendants and also radio to Jilin. The police must meet the train."

He found the attendants still whispering excitedly. He said, "No one is to enter or leave the car without my permission." They were also to quietly inform the attendants in the other cars of what had happened and enlist their help in surveillance. Lu knew this was not without risk considering the curiosity that was an intrinsic part of the Chinese character — probably, to be honest, of the human character, but it might result in some clue as to the murderer's identity. It occurred to him then to ask the attendants if they had seen anyone in the car who did not belong there.

"Yes, a Chinese man had been looking into the compartments."

"What a fool I am," thought Lu. "I should have asked them before." Still, he couldn't think of everything. This was a new situation for him. He reflected that Americans and Chinese certainly differed in nature. Americans often told more than anyone wanted to know. The Chinese, ever cautious, gave information only in response to direct questions. It was safer for them that way.

After getting a description of the stranger who had been peering into the compartments, Lu learned that the man had been seen a short time before Long Qiong had been assaulted but not after. Lu returned to consult with Rachel.

She had been looking through the papers in Mance's attache case. As Lu entered, she held out a piece of paper saying, "You will need to know about this. Would it help if I read it to you?"

"Yes, please, my reading is not well. I understand the speaking more than I can say. The reading is difficult."

Rachel could relate to that. She understood a good bit of spoken Chinese when she heard it, probably because of context; however, her ability to speak was quite limited, and her reading was confined to train and bus schedules, street signs, and menus. Even those often held some bewildering surprises.

The letter was in a spidery hand sprawled hastily across the page. The periods and commas were heavy slashes. It read:

Sidney,

Janice wrote to me last week to tell me about how you'd "thrown her over". She was devastated. I had to read the letter several times before I could even allow myself to understand what she meant. What have you done to her? It must have started even before I had left. For God's sake, how many women do you need?

I trusted you, believing that when I got back from China, we'd have a partnership, as you said, 'in every meaning of the word.' — that you would divorce Laura — move in with me and together we'd build the gallery and the life we'd talked about. Did you describe that life to Janice too?

I despise you for making a fool of me. How you must have laughed when you thought of Laura and me in the same town. But to seduce my little sister is too much. She said in her letter that she hasn't been able to concentrate. She's been skipping classes and is flunking out of school. You are to blame.

I see you now for what you really are, an egocentric bastard. I feel sorry for Laura. She's still married to you. At least I'm free of you.

Know this. Somehow I'll make you pay for your deceit and for hurting my sister. I don't know how, but I'll find a way.

M.

Lu looked thoughtful. "Mance *Xiansheng* was what you call unfaithful spouse?"

"I'm afraid so."

"And in America unfaithful men are sometimes murdered?"

"Well, sometimes, but neither Laura nor Melanie could ..." Rachel's voice trailed away as she pondered the implications.

"Nevertheless," Lu replied, "it is a motif."

"A motif? Oh, you mean a reason — a *motive*."

"Ah, yes, I mean a motive. We are gathering motives, correct?" He gave a shy smile. "Thank you for my improved English."

"This is mad," Rachel thought. "Here we sit next to a dead body discussing grammar and vocabulary." But she could not help feeling an affection for this earnest man who so much wanted to learn English. If anyone could get to the bottom of this horror, he could. She was sure of that.

"This Melanie, what of her?"

Rachel considered, trying to find the right words. Melanie was a beautiful Bette Midler type — outgoing, witty, lively. Rachel began, "She is very intelligent and funny, humorous. She was infatuated, that is, she imagined she was in love with Sidney Mance. Of course she was jealous of Laura Mance and plagued with uncertainty, especially because she felt guilty and also because she didn't hear from Sidney very often."

Lu interrupted, "Plagued, what is that?"

"Bothered, disturbed, upset. Please tell me if you don't understand everything I say."

Lu nodded.

"She confided, told me, about her unhappiness because of Sidney. Naturally, that made it difficult for me. I'm very fond of Laura too."

"But the letter says she will get even," Lu interposed.

"That's something anyone who is young and angry might say. Melanie doesn't have a mean bone in her body."

"What is this *mean bone*?"

"I mean she couldn't have hurt anyone. She isn't capable of doing that."

Lu had a faraway look in his eyes as though dredging up scenes from the past. He said slowly, "Madam, anyone is able to hurt another immensely."

The grave certainty of his pronouncement shook Rachel. She supposed he was right, but these young people — none of them could — could they?

Lu had pulled a notebook from his pocket to jot things down. His hastily written characters were, nevertheless, beautifully formed. They had what Rachel's calligraphy teacher would call *soul force*. They reflected the inner person of Lu Xing.

"Tell me about Mance *Furen*," Lu asked.

"Laura ... I think Laura is pregnant, going to have a baby."

"Ah," said Lu. "Mr. Mance must have been very happy."

Rachel didn't respond. "I can't do this to my friend," she thought. "I just can't."

Lu studied her and tried to weigh his next words carefully. "You are not telling me something I need to know. If your friends are innocent, what you say to me will not hurt them, truly, I promise you."

Rachel hesitated, then finally said, "I don't think Sidney Mance is, was, the father."

"Truly?" Lu Xing's eyebrows made a little tent of astonishment. "Who is the father?"

Rachel inhaled and sighed, "It could be Frank Li."

"But he is a Chinese!" Shock and disapproval registered on Lu's face.

"Nevertheless, I think I'm right."

"Ah, ah," Lu shook his head sadly preparing himself to think beyond this moral hurdle. "And Li, why do you call him Frank?"

"Most of our Chinese students ask for Western names. I know he isn't a student, but when Laura was naming her students, he asked her if she would call him Frank. It seems his mother had heard some old Frank Sinatra songs somewhere, so he thought Frank would be a good name. His real name is Li Guanghai. As a fellow teacher in the English department at the university, he naturally spent time with all of us. He offered to accompany Laura on short trips to serve as her interpreter. They — a— became fond of each other. But Frank is another person who just couldn't have ..."
Rachel stopped when she saw Lu's stern look. "All right," she said. "In theory, anyone can murder if the provocation is sufficient. But I can't believe it about any of these young people, Frank, Laura, Melanie or Paul. I just can't believe it!"

She couldn't stand to think about it any longer. She suddenly blurted out, "And please don't call me, Madam."

Lu Xing blinked in astonishment at her outburst. These Americans were so unpredictable.

"I'm sorry." said Rachel feeling foolish. She was ashamed that she had become angry with this delightful man just because she was concerned about her friends. "It's hard to explain, but madam is just not what I wish to be called."

Lu looked apologetic. He must have made a grave error. His old British book on conversational English definitely said *Madam*. Perhaps that wasn't the American way. "But to say the first name is too difficult, too familiar. What shall I say?" He thought for a moment, then with a pleased look he said, "Rachel *Laoshi*, teacher Rachel. You are a teacher. You are my teacher. *Laoshi* (teacher) is a word of respect. May I call you Rachel *Laoshi* — the first name with respect?"

Rachel was touched by his sensitivity. If only her American students had such respect. She was certainly spoiled after teaching in China. Here her students carried her parcels. They erased the board after her classes. They listened to everything she said! The throes of The Cultural Revolution had not been able to wipe out all of the old in China. The Confucian virtues which had been a pervasive influence in Chinese society for over two thousand years apparently were too ingrained to be removed. Respect for elders, respect for learning, a hierarchy in which each person was static in his or her position in society, were ideas which were hard to change. True, there was much that could be considered wrong with this concept, but it had been a stabilizing influence in a society un-wieldy due to sheer numbers and distances alone. What would a move toward democracy bring? Less stability to be sure. Rachel hoped that the good would not be jettisoned along with the bad in the Chinese attempt to be prosperous and modern.

Lu was looking at her expectantly.

"Rachel *Laoshi* is very good," she said. "It pleases me."

Lu smiled with relief. "To the business," he said. "Tell me about this Paul, the young man with the curly hair."

"Paul Solomon. He has also confided in me. He loves Melanie, truly loves her. Somehow he knows about her affair with Mance. I don't know. Perhaps she told him herself. Anyway, of course he was angry with Mance. He thought Melanie would come to her senses some time, and he intended to be there waiting. He is sar-donic and sarcastic, but, in actual fact, seems to be a very vulner-able young man."

Lu raised his hand to stop her. "That means... ?"

Rachel thought for a minute. "I'm not sure I can explain. It means that he sees everything that is wrong in society. He would like it to be right, but he pretends to be so wise that he knows things can't be that way. Consequently, he makes comments that are mean, sometimes petty. In reality, he believes that the ideals of communism are good — sharing goods equally, taking care of the weak and the poor in the community. He's not religious in the strictest sense of the word, but he likes to point out the similarities between Christian and Communist tenets. There is a quotation from the Christian Bible that I have heard him use over and over again in this argument. It is:

> 'There was not a needy person among them, for
> as many as were possessors of land or houses sold
> them, and brought the proceeds of what was sold
> and laid it at the apostles' feet; and distribution was
> made to each as any had need.'

It is from the book of Acts in the New Testament.

I suppose Paul thinks an ideal society is possible and he is angry with people that they haven't achieved it."

"Do you?" Lu asked.

"Do I what?"

"Believe that an ideal society is possible."

"No," Rachel said firmly.

Lu shook his head sadly looking at the blanketed body. "It is only for young people to believe — and dreamers."

Rachel thought of Phil. He was neither young nor a dreamer, but somehow he was able to retain a belief in perfectibility. It wasn't that, intellectually, Phil did not understand the enormous amount of evil in the world. It was just that he seemed not to be aware of it as being within himself. Rachel was acquainted with her darker side. She hoped it was small enough to be managed always; however, her awareness of it made her realize the truth of Lu's statement that *anyone is able to hurt another immensely.*

She imagined that Lu and all those who had survived the Cultural Revolution had been forced to confront their darker sides head on. The nervous giggle with which most Chinese responded to mention of that time was a means of shying away from that confrontation. Rachel knew that Confucius had begun with the premise that goodness was a virtue that could be ordered by intellect and tradition. The Western Judeo-Christian premise began with the certainty of the existence of evil. From there it had developed law to circumscribe the evil and render it less potent. Whether from experience or belief, both the East and the West knew how easily the dark side could erupt, even in the heart of those who are good.

Chapter 12

"We must begin our questions." Lu said. "I will talk to the soldiers in the last compartment. Perhaps they will happily move to another car. Then we can use their space to deduce."

Rachel looked at the blanketed body opposite her. "Happily or not," she thought, "I hope they will move." She smiled at Lu Xing. "That would make *me* very happy — very."

"Will you speak with the teachers from Changchun in the second compartment? Find what they noticed before the first tunnel and before the next."

After Lu left, Rachel sat there for a moment. She was trying to prepare herself mentally for the interview. It wasn't so much that she disliked these people as individuals. But she did dislike their attitude that they, and they alone, had the answers to how others should think and believe. She had to face it. She had a strong prejudice against them. She felt that their goal of *saving souls for Christ*, which was disguised by their willingness to teach English in China, was deplorably dishonest and arrogant.

She knew that an indigenous Christian Church called the Three Self Movement was developing in China. Under the recently more relaxed communism, all religions were reemerging. The basic premise of the Three Self Movement was that its members should be self governing — no denominational ties to the West and former missionary movements—, self propagating, and self financing. These goals made sense to Rachel. About one percent of the Chinese people now belonged to this church. The members did many things for their fellow Chinese that the government was no longer willing or able to do. The church had established nursing homes for the elderly who had no families; it had started workshops where the handicapped were able to manufacture goods and receive wages, and it sponsored *barefoot doctors* to serve the remote rural population. Ironically, the church now embodied many of the ideals of taking care of the people that communism had espoused in its early years. Naturally, regional governments were anxious to work with the local branches of the church. Most of these Christians were well respected by the other Chinese people as being honest people and good citizens.

China's past had been filled with episode after episode when many alien practices and attitudes were imposed on it by Westerners. Once again it seemed, Westerners such as the Changchun teachers, were trying to tell the Chinese people what would be *best* for them. Well, enough of these reflections, or she would work herself into a state of indignation that would certainly be unproductive in finding the murderer. A small doubt crept into Rachel's mind as she pondered whether *her* motives for being in China could bear intense scrutiny. Just why was she here?

The teachers from the university in Changchun, Sissy and Stephen Turner and Marcie and John Morrison, were seated with their *waiban*, Zhu Liangxu. Rachel wondered briefly if he had been persuaded to *see the light.*

She poked her head into their compartment. Clearing her throat, she said, "May I come in and talk to you for a moment?"

"Of course, of course," several of them answered. Then Marcie Morrison said with disingenuous air, "About anything special?"

"As a matter of fact, yes," replied Rachel, "about the murder."

Immediately, the American faces assumed the sepulchral looks appropriate to the coming conversation. They began moving possessions and squeezing together to clear the sixth space for Rachel.

"He was the husband of the young teacher at your school, wasn't he?" asked Sissy. "The man who was murdered, I mean ..."

"Yes."

John Morrison spoke up, "None of us knew him, so there's really not much we can tell you."

"I, that is, we assumed that," replied Rachel. "You see, I'm helping the train detective, Lu Xing. Basically, what we need to know is whether you might have noticed where the various occupants of this car were before Long Qiong (that's my *waiban*) was assaulted and also before Sidney Mance was murdered — or, for that matter, anything unusual afterwards too."

"Ah, we understand," Stephen said. "But we were all together both times," he looked at the others for confirmation, " ... at least we were all within sight of each other." He was clearly the leader of the group and was anxious to set the record straight.

Rachel smiled at them and said, "I don't think that any of you are seriously being considered as possible suspects, but your help would be greatly appreciated."

Stephen nodded. Then he looked at the others as if to say, "Here is your task. Now think." They thought.

John Morrison was the first to speak. " I remember that I was sitting on one of the jump seats in the aisle looking out the window shortly before we came to the second tunnel. I'd needed to move around a little. The young Chinese teacher, the man, came out of the last compartment at the other end next to the toilet. He passed me carrying a thermos and stopped outside the attendants' room. About then I went back into our compartment and had just sat down again when the train went through the tunnel. I think someone was coming down the aisle to my right, but frankly, I wasn't paying any particular attention and I might be mistaken. I'm not sure where anyone was when the murder was discovered. Everyone just seemed to appear in the aisle." He turned to look at his companions. "Do any of you remember anything then?" They all shook their heads no. Everyone lapsed into silence again.

Marcie looked thoughtful. "I think," she said, "Yes, I'm sure that I saw the tall redhead walk by our compartment and go through the door beyond the attendants' compartment onto the platform."

"When was that?" Rachel asked.

"Oh, that wasn't before the murder. It was just before we went through the first tunnel. It was so confusing both times. When they found your *waiban* hurt — and then the murder — and with all those antiques around him. It's awful — like a judgment of God." Much to Rachel's astonishment Marcie began to quote: "This night thy soul shall be required of thee; ..." However, Marcie broke off abruptly when she looked at Rachel's glowering face.

Rachel was having no sessions of quoting scripture, true though it might be. She gritted her teeth and spoke with some dispatch. "Is there anything else anyone can think of that might help?"

No one had anything to add; however, they all assured her they would give it more thought, and they would definitely pray for the soul of Sidney Mance.

As Rachel was leaving their compartment, Lu Xing hailed her from the next doorway. "My comrades in the military feel their duty strongly; therefore, they have gone, with the help of the train attendants, to the next compartment. Come into 'our office'. We must compare our discoveries. I have also talked to the Japanese ladies through their *waiban*, Gui Shijie. I have some information from them. We will now prepare the diagrams."

"Diagrams?" questioned Rachel as she wondered if they were taking a break for another English lesson.

"We will draw the train car like this." With a flourish, he produced a paper on which the train car with all its compartments had been drawn neatly. "We will put the people where we know them for each time — the hitting of Long Qiong and the murder of Sidney Mance. Then we will begin to discover things."

"I hope so," said Rachel dubiously.

She learned from Lu Xing that just before Long Qiong was assaulted, Paul had been seen alone in the compartment he and Melanie shared. Two of the military men had been smoking outside the empty compartment while they waited their turns to use the toilet. They had casually glanced into Paul's compartment next to the empty one. The third soldier was in the toilet at the time. This was confirmed by Rachel's information that Marcie Morrison had seen Melanie go through to the platform at about the same time. Paul and Melanie were not together during the first incident.

"So, said Lu Xing, "both don't have the alibis."

"Right," agreed Rachel. "We also know that both Long Qiong and Sidney Mance were alone. In fact, it seems that everyone was alone except for George Kim, Claire Lucas and me. We were all together on the other platform at that time. And Laura Mance and Frank Li were in the dining car when I was there. I left first. I know they couldn't have passed me even when the train was going through the tunnel.

Of course, there are the military men, the Japanese girls and their *waiban* and the teachers from Changchun to account for, but I think we can pretty much eliminate them as suspects; don't you? You haven't found any connection between any of them and either Sidney or Long Qiong have you?"

"No, for now we will think they cannot have done it. If they connect with either Long Qiong or Mance, we will think again. OK?"

"So, now what? What do you think the murder weapon was?"

Lu Xing stroked the side of his face. "I'm saying that the weapon was tossed out the window. Nothing of the correct shape was in the compartment by the body, and the window was open. It must have been a round and heavy thing."

"Could a woman have committed the murder?"

"To be sure. With both assaults, the stroke fell from the upper air — above."

"What about searching the compartments?" Rachel asked.

"We will wait. My mind says the weapon is gone — out the window. What other thing do we know to look for?"

"True," conceded Rachel. They didn't know why Long Qiong had been attacked or Sidney murdered, but it seemed logical that the two must be connected.

"We will visit George Kim in his compartment. Claire Lucas is still with Mrs. Mance, correct?"

"Yes, I think so," Rachel said as she took one more look at their charts. Were they getting anywhere? Maybe.

Chapter 13

"Yes I would rather see Kim in his own compartment," said Lu Xing, talking mainly to himself. "I'm not sure why, but maybe something will be telling."

When Lu and Rachel entered into Kim's apartment, he was leaning back in the seat staring at the ceiling fan with an intense concentration. They asked if they could talk to him. He inclined his head in agreement and gestured to the opposite seat which was piled with papers. Lu Xing moved some of the clutter so that he and Rachel could sit down. As he stacked things in a heap in the corner, Lu glanced idly at what he was moving. There were magazines on fashion, Western and Hong Kong newspapers, brochures on silk, a large pocket dictionary and a sack of Chinese cookies. He took the opportunity to study George casually as he accomplished his tidying. He looked carefully at George's safari jacket. As he had noticed before, it bulged with all kinds of paraphernalia, but there were no signs of blood stains on the sleeves or anywhere else. It was only negative evidence at best. The wound on Sidney Mance's head had not bled very much. Kim's pants and shoes were dark, but Lu Xing couldn't detect any recent stains on them. He would have liked to search Kim's compartment, but he concluded that it would be a futile effort. He didn't know what, if anything, he should be looking for.

Kim seemed relaxed, but there was a certain alertness about him that belied his posture. He spoke idly as he continued to look at the fan.

"Strange, the ceiling fan is working," he said. "I always find it interesting when something *is* working in this country. So often things don't, you know." He finally turned his attention to them both giving them an appraising look. "Do you think you'll get to the bottom of this?" he asked.

Lu was also making an estimate of Kim. What kind of man was he? What questions would be best to get him talking? Lu decided on a straight forward approach. "Did you like Sidney Mance?" he asked.

Kim looked as though the question of like or dislike had never occurred to him. With a surprising frankness he replied, "Now that you've asked, no, I suppose not. Still, I did do business with him. I'm the one who suggested it to him — that I look for antiques while I was traveling here for my business. It seemed to add another dimension to my trips — more like a treasure hunt. There was always that marvelous find that might be waiting for me in the next town."

"And did you ever find that marvelous thing?"

"I've certainly found some handsome objects for Sidney, things he never could have found himself, but, no, nothing too spectacular."

Rachel looked at Lu. He nodded. She said to Kim, "I talked to Lu Xing about the afternoon I meet you, Claire and Sidney at Beishan Park. I told him about the awful comment Sidney made about Broken Back Bridge and the people who died there."

"Yes," Kim agreed. "I was extremely angry. Still, a person doesn't kill someone because of a stupid remark, no matter how offensive."

"Was Mance honest with you in his business dealings?" Lu asked.

George laughed, "I found early on that he had tried to cheat me. I told him that I would take my finds somewhere else if he ever tried it again."

"What were the terms of the agreement between you and Mance?" Rachel asked.

"As I said, I had approached him. I told him I could find Chinese and Korean antiques for him that he hadn't a hope of ever finding himself. I didn't have access to buyers in the States, so we needed each other. I told him I wanted forty percent of the selling price of each item. At first he balked and tried to get me down to thirty percent; however, when I showed him some things I had already picked up, he realized that I knew what I was doing. He agreed to forty."

"And the time he did cheat. How did you know?" inquired Lu.

"When I enter any business for the first time, I always make it a point to get to know the assistants or the secretary well. It's like having another key to the door. And Claire, well you may have noticed, she's an attractive, sophisticated woman. I knew it would be good to know her."

"So you cultivated her," said Rachel trying not to sound too judgmental.

"Yes, you could call it that." George laughed again. "I've never wanted to be tied down, so I've never had the urge to marry, but that doesn't mean I don't have urges. Claire is very pleasant and convenient, and she has certainly been in a position to keep track of Sidney Mance's sales for me."

Rachel wondered what Claire would think of this cavalier description of her relationship to George. Not much, she was sure.

Lu was aware of the angry edge to Rachel's voice. He didn't want George Kim to be too much on the defensive — maybe later, but not right now. He decided to intervene.

"Would you tell us more about the comment Sidney made about your mother?" Lu asked.

Kim gave Lu Xing a long level look. "I don't see that it has any significance," he said flatly.

Lu Xing did not respond. Both men, suspect and interrogator, lapsed into a silence which took them into past experiences that Rachel could merely try to imagine. The world of conformity of the Cultural Revolution held raw memories for each which, despite their personal dissimilarities, bound them together in a strange way.

They both saw the millions of figures in blue or grey twill pants, blue Mao jackets and blue caps which transformed the Chinese people into hives of indistinguishable worker ants scurrying around apprehensively, prepared to sacrifice any part of selfhood in order to gain the safety of mediocre anonymity.

Kim tried not to think of that time. Thinking held untold dangers, but his mind would not obey him. That terrible time — his mother — He had become more and more worried about her. She seemed constantly preoccupied and unhappy. At times, she barely noticed that he existed. He had felt an urgent need to protect her — to say something to her, but what did a young boy know to say to his mother? What could he say that would make any difference? He didn't even understand what the trouble was.

She had walked around their apartment looking haunted as though there were horrors lurking in every corner. Early in the mornings, he had often seen her through the doorway sitting on the edge of the bed with her head hanging down. She looked so incapable of movement that he was afraid she might never take that first step.

It had been a time when people avoided looking into each others' eyes. They hurried back and forth doing what they had to without really making human contact — avoiding everything they could possibly avoid.

One day his mother had come home from work looking even more distraught than usual. After dinner, she had put her arms around him briefly without saying a word. It was like having the arms of someone who was dead encircling him. He was terrified. They went to bed early that evening. He listened for her every breath and sigh. Later, he heard her moving around the room stealthily. He guessed that she was preparing to go out. He was afraid to breathe for fear that she would know he was awake. She moved quickly and quietly. The outside door opened and closed. As soon as she was outside, he scrambled out of bed and began searching the floor for his woven straw shoes. Although it was a bitterly cold evening, he didn't even think about the temperature. He thrust his bare feet into the shoes, grabbed an over shirt and ran to follow her.

His mother's death was like thousands of stories from that time. The detective, Lu Xing, would know. But this American teacher? She could hear the story, but she would never understand. Stupid acts of cruelty— useless — but the stories were so similar that it was hard to distinguish one from another unless it happened to be your story.

Finally, Kim spoke to Lu Xing and Rachel. "My mother was continually harassed at work. I'm not sure why. As our illustrious leader, Chairman Mao said, 'If a nail sticks up above the others, pound it in.' My mother must have been such a protruding nail. Eventually it became too much for her to endure. I didn't begin to understand; I only know that committing suicide must have seemed the best way out for her. I was angry with her for leaving me, and I was angry at the world which made it happen. Sidney Mance's ignorance of those times infuriated me."

"And what did you do after her death?" Lu Xing asked.

Again there was no answer. Kim stared out of the window, but his eyes were turned inward. Lu Xing did not push him to speak.

George Kim continued to relive that night. He willed his memories to stop, but they poured into his consciousness with the rush of a volcanic eruption.

George had followed his mother, but not closely enough. He had thought she might be going to the temple on Beishan to pray. True, it was forbidden, but he knew many people were willing to take the risk. They seemed to need something more than the mean drudgery of their everyday lives.

He would always see her body rushing downward through the air from the bridge above to fall onto the cement path only yards in front of him. What happened next was something he could permit himself to see only as an onlooker as though he were watching a play. He did not dare to feel it.

He saw a young boy kneeling beside the twisted body, howling grief like an animal baying the moon. He saw another figure, a nun from the temple, slip quietly from the shadows and coax the boy to his feet. He saw the boy being led, almost dragged, away by the nun with the soft voice who took him through a hole at the base of the temple walls into a room where straw and blankets were piled into one corner. He remembered the boy lying there sobbing, ashamed to be alive, ashamed to be touched by the moonlight which spilled its white light into strange patterns through the unpaned windows.

He stayed there for several months, hiding during the day and waiting at night for the nun who was secretly tending the temple to return from her daytime job in the textile factory. Some nights she held him until he stopped shaking and fell asleep. When he awoke in the morning, she was always gone, but he could see the comforting impression of her small body in the pile of straw and blankets not far away.

After a few weeks, he became enough aware of the world again to make secret expeditions outside the temple complex to forage for food in the surrounding countryside. He became an accomplished thief. He and the nun often ate as well as the most highly placed cadres.

When the weather turned cold and winter seemed about to set in, he was strong enough to begin his journey away from the nightmare. He traveled South. Bit by bit, he discarded the boy he had been and took up a new persona, that of an affable con man. He found that the skills and the callousness needed for this role came easily. After a number of months, he stowed away on a ship headed for Seoul, Korea. When the ship docked, he sought out the home of his uncle. By willing it, he had caused the boy, Kim Myun Hee to die. In his place, George Kim was created. His mother, Jilin, and Broken Back Bridge had been sealed in a box. He had not opened it again until this past week.

While he was visiting the Beishan Temple Fair with Mance, Claire Lucas and the American teachers, he had looked for his nun. He saw her kneeling in front of an altar piled high with all kinds of fruits, vegetables and meats which were offerings from the people attending the fair. Although she must now be in her seventies, her unlined face seemed almost as young as the faces of the group of acolytes who knelt beside her. If she had seen George, she would not have recognized him. But he would always know her. He was glad to see from the bounty on the altar that she would still be eating well. They had both, in their own ways, become survivors.

Kim again became aware of the two people who waited patiently for a response. "I made my way to my uncle's home in Korea. From there I eventually went to America. That is all."

"Did Claire Lucas like Sidney Mance?" asked Rachel abruptly.

George smiled slowly, "I rather think not."

"Why not?" inquired Lu Xing.

"Don't ask me to tell you, but you might want to check with Claire about what happened between Sidney and her mother. That's all I can tell you, really. I don't know why Sidney was murdered; however, I'm sure you will find any number of reasons." Again, he laughed, rather bitterly.

As he stood in the doorway of Kim's compartment preparing to leave, Lu Xing turned back to look at Kim. "Where were you when Sidney Mance was murdered?"

"In my compartment with Claire. Just ask her."

"To be sure," said Lu. "I will."

102

When they had left Kim, Rachel turned to Lu and asked, "What do you think?"

"I think he is a complicating man. Correct?"

Rachel smiled, "He may very well be complicating, but you would call him a *complicated man* or a *complex man*."

"Ah, I see," said Lu. "Very good. It is too soon to conclude about Kim. We must continue gathering information."

"Who next?"

"I am thinking Paul Solomon and then the Hazen woman. We will see what they have to say." Lu turned to Rachel and said, "I must ask you an important thing. I know Mance *Furen* is to be called Mrs. Mance. I know Solomon is called Mr. Solomon, but what do I call the other females who are not married?"

"Ms.," said Rachel.

"Mizz," repeated Lu Xing as he tried the word on his tongue. "Mizz like the buzz of a bee. Correct?"

"Yes, but not quite so strong a buzz."

"Hah, very interesting. You are a Ms.?"

"Yes, if you didn't call me Rachel *Laoshi*, you would call me Ms. Toussant. However, I'm to be married when I return to the States. I haven't decided yet whether to keep this name or take my new husband's name. I've had this name for such a long time."

"To be married, excellent!" Lu clapped his hands together. "May I ask you to convey my warmly felt congratulations to the most lucky man?"

"I'll be glad to do that," Rachel responded with a wry grin. "Now, shall we ask Mr. Solomon to visit us?"

"Yes, we must learn everything." Lu replied seriously.

Chapter 14

Paul Solomon was not happy at being summoned to answer questions. He entered the compartment sullenly, plopped himself in a corner as far away from Rachel and Lu Xing as possible, folded his arms tightly across his chest, and glared at Rachel.

His fierce expression made her decidedly uncomfortable. It was plain that Paul now considered her to be a defector to the *adversarial side.* Even though she had great affection for him, it was a fondness often tinged with exasperation at his pigheaded attitudes. He didn't tolerate opposition easily. He was a young man who constantly espoused great love for the masses of humanity. He had definite theoretical ideas about how governments could serve the people; yet he had rather sizable difficulties loving and getting along with individual fellow humans.

Lu Xing didn't seem at all perturbed by Paul's attitude. He remained silent displaying a serene patience while he waited to see what Paul would do.

Finally, Paul broke the silence with a snort of contempt. "Well, fire away. I'm ready."

Lu looked at him directly. "I must ask you where you were and what you were doing when the *waiban*, Long Qiong was hurt."

"I was in our compartment, of course ... with Melanie."

"You are sure?"

"Certainly, why should I lie?"

"Why indeed?" countered Lu skeptically. "And when Sidney Mance was murdered ... ?"

"Again, Melanie and I were together in our compartment."

"Please think," said Lu. "You do not wish to change what you have said?"

"No, damn it. That's it."

"Ah ... then I will record what you have said," responded Lu as he wrote rapidly in his notebook. "And what did you do? What did you talk about?"

"How in the world do you expect me to remember that? — things — our students — how frustrating the Chinese officials can be — I don't know. Ask Melanie."

"I will. You were aware that Melanie threatened Sidney Mance, were you not?"

Paul threw Rachel a look of disgust. Lu understood the look and spoke rapidly. "No, Rachel *Laoshi* did not betray her. I have found a letter that Melanie sent to Sidney. In it, she makes the threats. Perhaps you know of this letter." Lu Xing held it up, but did not hand it to Paul.

Paul fell silent. Rachel could almost hear the wheels turning in his head.

"Look," Paul said, "of course Melanie was angry. The bastard had seduced her kid sister after he and Melanie had ..." His voice trailed off as though he couldn't stand to talk about what Melanie and Sidney had done.

"Had an affair?" suggested Lu.

"Yes, right, but you have to remember that Melanie is very young, impressionable. She was probably flattered by the kind of attention an older man could give her. Besides, he had money and used it lavishly when it suited him. She would have gotten, was getting, over him. She was angry, sure, but whatever she said, she couldn't have killed Sidney. I know her. Melanie couldn't have done it."

"And you?" asked Lu Xing. "Could you have done it?"

"If you're thinking I killed him, there's no way! That would have been really stupid."

"But you do love Melanie very much, don't you?" asked Rachel.

Paul's face assumed an expression which held a mixture of embarrassment, irritation and confidence.

"Yes, I love her, and she does like me, you know. I'm sure she'll forget him and everything will be all right."

Lu Xing looked at Paul thoughtfully. "Naturally, now that your rival is dead, Melanie will find you more to her liking. It *is* good for you that he's dead, correct?"

"Yeah, I'm glad. Is that what you want me to say? But not glad enough to have killed him. Get real!"

"But if you love her so truly ...?" said Lu.

"No," said Paul adamantly in a loud voice. "I told you she would have gotten over him. I certainly didn't need to kill him to make her come to her senses. His affair with her sister did that. She wasn't interested in him anymore. She was just angry."

"And she wanted to get the revenge? And you were angry for her?" queried Lu.

Paul turned to Rachel, opening both hands in an exasperated plea for understanding.

"Rachel," he said, "Please tell this guy how things are. You know for me to kill Sidney would have been insane, at least for the reasons he is suggesting. Now if I had wanted to do the world a service — well, that's another story."

Rachel spoke to Paul as though he were a little boy. "Paul, this is serious. If you persist in being flippant, people will misunderstand you. I know you and what you're like, but others don't."

Paul opened his mouth and then closed it without saying anything. He looked somewhat chastened. Rachel turned to Lu and said, "I'm afraid Paul is right. It just isn't enough of a motive."

"If he wanted to protect Ms. Hazen, then he might; is that not so?" argued Lu.

Paul merely rolled his eyes toward the ceiling and shook his head emphatically back and forth. "No, no, no," he said.

Lu raised both hands. "Enough," he said. "I think perhaps you did not kill him, but I still have suspicions that you may be protecting Ms. Hazen. I must warn you. I know that you were not together when Long Qiong was hit."

"How do you know that?" challenged Paul.

"You were seen alone in the compartment by one group. Ms. Hazen was seen somewhere else by Mrs. Morrison. If you lied about that, you could just as well have lied about the time of Mance's murder."

"Hah, Mrs. Morrison, one of our religious friends — well, you certainly would have to believe her; wouldn't you? What can I say? All right, we weren't together when Long Qiong was attacked, but we definitely were when Sidney was put out of his misery."

Rachel saw that her lecture about being flippant had had no effect. Lu Xing just gave Paul a skeptical look.

"We shall see," he said. "If you do not know any more which is helpful, for now, we shall stop." He looked at Paul with a question in his eyes.

"Nothing." said Paul.

"Then you are free to go, but I must ask that you wait here until Rachel *Laoshi* fetches Ms. Hazen to this compartment. I don't want you to make comparing notes. Do you understand?"

Paul gave a mock bow of acknowledgment as Rachel left the compartment to get Melanie. When the two women returned, Paul gave Melanie a wink and a *thumbs up* gesture. Then he disappeared into the aisle whistling "Some Enchanted Evening."

Chapter 15

When they had finished talking to Paul, Rachel brought Melanie Hazen into the compartment. Melanie was in a state of skittish fright as though she might break into any manner of wild behavior in an instant. Lu Xing decided to take advantage of her unstable mood. With a flourish, he produced her letter to Mance and laid it on the table in front of her with a slapping motion.

Melanie looked at it; then she blanched visibly.

"You had great reason to be angry with Sidney Mance. Is that not correct?" he said very sternly.

She began to cry, resulting in much snuffling and clanging of bracelets.

Lu continued to press his advantage. "I must insist that you answer me." he said in a cold voice.

Melanie tore absently at a wad of Kleenex that Rachel had handed her. She looked past Lu's right shoulder at the heavily stained lace antimacassar, which was standard issue for protecting the seats on Chinese trains, as though she might draw some inspiration from it. Nothing was forthcoming.

Unexpectedly she said, "Sidney was a shit!" with an expulsion of breath on the last word. "But Paul and I were together in our compartment all the time. Surely he told you that; didn't he?" With that question she looked directly into Lu Xing's eyes challenging him.

Lu chose not to answer. Rachel watched Melanie's progressive disintegration with growing dismay.

"Paul said you were also together when Long Qiong was assaulted," Lu added.

"That's right," Melanie said in an unsure voice.

Lu pressed in to attack. "It is most certainly not true. You have both lied. You were seen going to the platform beyond the attendants' room at the time Long Qiong was assaulted. You were by yourself and so was Paul."

"Who? who said I was there?" Melanie wailed.

"It is of no importance. The witness is to be trusted. You both say you were also together when Sidney was murdered. Why should you be believed?"

"But it is true! Oh, it is. We were together then. How can I make you believe it?"

Lu gave her a steady look. "I'm afraid you can't," he said dryly.

Melanie looked to Rachel for help. Rachel felt wretched about her position in this whole thing. She said somewhat lamely. "Melanie, just try to be as clear as you can about things. I'm sure it will be all right." But she wasn't at all sure. All she was sure of was that her relationships with these young people of whom she was so fond was being inevitably altered.

"Damn, Sidney," she thought. "If ever a victim was to blame, he was."

"Perhaps you and Paul worked together to kill Sidney." Lu speculated.

"No, no," cried Melanie in exasperation, "That's absurd."

"What did you mean when you said *I'll make you pay for your deceit*"? Lu asked continuing relentlessly.

"Oh, God, the letter. It was a stupid threat which didn't really mean anything. If I had ever been in a position to do Sidney harm like spoil a business deal or something — ruin one of his many romances, I'd have certainly done that, but I didn't mean anything like murder."

"And Paul, he loves you much; am I right? And he was angry with Sidney also because of that?" Lu said.

"Paul always seems more fierce than he is. He wouldn't hurt a soul. He just likes to pretend to be the *angry young man*. I'm convinced that he'll grow out of it. Paul yells and blusters at everybody, but he wouldn't physically harm anyone." Melanie gave a little half smile at the thought of Paul. The smile wasn't lost on either Rachel or Lu Xing.

"Perhaps, you will be thinking he is more *your cup of tea* now, hum?" said Lu trying to disguise the mischief in his eyes.

"Perhaps you are right," said Melanie reflecting.

Lu became stern again. "Do not think we have finished. We will get to the bottom of this. Can you tell me of anything about the others that might seem odd to you?"

There was a pause while Melanie pulled herself together and began to concentrate on something other than her own woes. She frowned and said, "Now that you ask, Sidney did seem impervious to the daggers I was sending him." She clapped a hand over her mouth as she realized that her choice of words for metaphor could be completely misconstrued by this man.

Rachel smoothly inserted an explanation. She said, "Impervious means not able to be influenced by. That is, Melanie is saying that Sidney didn't seem to notice her anger. Sending daggers means giving him angry looks. She didn't mean anything more than that. It's just something we say." Her voice trailed off rather inconclusively.

Lu was trying to assimilate all this. It was good to have a teacher, but there was so much to learn so quickly. He tried to assume a sage expression. "I see," he pronounced gravely. He had all but eliminated Melanie as a serious killer, but it wouldn't do to let her know that. He might gain much valuable information from her if he could frighten her just enough to make her respectful.

Yes, he was certainly learning much from this close contact with these Americans. They came in a variety of types. He would never be able to stereotype them again. In the short time he had known Rachel Toussant, he had gained respect for her intelligence and her good intentions, but he was dubious as to whether she would have survived very long during the Cultural Revolution. She was definitely not a political creature. Everything that she thought was telegraphed instantly onto her face. She could be read like a map. Therefore, he had to be careful about letting her know exactly whom he suspected. He was sure she would unintentionally give the culprit ample warning. Then he thought ruefully, "No problem. I suspect almost everyone. I don't seem to be making much progress in narrowing things down." It was with a sinking feeling that he returned to interviewing Melanie.

"And in addition to Sidney— what about the others? Are they different?" he asked.

Again, Melanie paused to think. "I haven't noticed anything unusual. Of course, I don't know George Kim or Claire Lucas well enough to tell. Most of us just met them recently. I'm certain there is nothing else I can tell you."

Lu looked at her steadily. "I need the help of all of you. Now go, please. Talk to Paul and stay in your compartment unless you think of something important to tell me. Then I will expect you must tell me. Will you be sure to do that?"

"Yes, if we think of anything, we'll let you know immediately."

As she left the compartment, Melanie looked down at Lu from her towering six-foot height, but her demeanor was that of a chastened little girl. She said, "I couldn't murder anyone. Please believe me." She wiped away the remnants of her tears, and then, squaring her shoulders, headed back to her compartment. She didn't say a word to Rachel who was now apparently to be considered a member of the enemy camp.

" You were awfully hard on her," complained Rachel.

"I know, but we must be certain where everyone was."

"Can you honestly imagine that she might have done it?"

Lu smiled, "My instinct (is that the right word?) whispers in my ear, *it is not she,* but I must be sure. Melanie is most assuredly a big, strong woman capable of pounding anyone's head."

Rachel laughed because she was relieved by the news that Lu didn't consider Melanie a likely suspect. She could also picture Melanie pounding someone's head which made a very funny image.

"You're right. She could deliver quite a blow if necessary, but I can't believe she would. Besides, we would have heard her bracelets."

Lu laughed at her joke, but then he became serious again.
"Ah," he said, "You lack the realistic nature. You cannot believe anyone committed the murder."

Rachel was a little offended by his pronouncement. "I didn't say that at all," she countered defensively.

Lu was looking preoccupied again. He asked, "Do all young, modern American ladies say, *shit?*"

With a bit of embarrassment, Rachel shrugged her shoulders. "I'm afraid many do," she answered.

Chapter 16

Rachel was beginning to feel like a pariah. She could only hope that her friends would be able to forgive her when this was over. She fully understood Lu's argument. To do justice to the others, the murderer must be found. Unfortunately, the search meant opening a number of cans of worms. She hated being the person doing that.

The next logical step was to question Laura Mance and Frank Li, but she had no stomach for it. Surely Lu Xing could manage without her this time. As she opened her mouth to speak, Lu interrupted her.

"I know you are thinking again about friendship. I understand. Helping me is difficult, but I need your help, most assuredly. You see, already I am reading your mind."

"If you could read other people's minds as well," she thought grumpily, "we might have solved this by now."

She said, pointedly, "Despite everything else, it *is* Laura's husband who is dead."

"Umh, maybe it will be best if we question Mrs. Mance and Mr. Li together. How do you think?"

Rachel didn't even bother correcting his grammar.

"Like I want out," she said to herself; however, she could see that Lu expected her to be rational about fulfilling the task he had assigned to her.

"Could we go to their compartment?" she asked.

"Yes, we will see them there." Lu poured a cup of tea from his thermos and handed it to Rachel. "Maybe this will help." As he offered the tea, Lu was acutely aware of the urgent need to move ahead quickly with the questioning. Having traveled this train line often, he recognized that Jilin was not much more than an hour away, but he was even more concerned with being in the right frame of mind to question Laura Mance and Frank Li. He knew himself well enough to have learned that, on the few times he had permitted prejudice or emotion to rule his mind, he had made grave mistakes. He must be able to pick up any nuances without having them clouded by his feelings about the people he was dealing with.

In the case of Frank Li, that would be difficult. He didn't know the man, but he thought he understood the type. There were some Chinese who would sell their very souls to get to America. Lu had been shocked when Rachel suggested that Li might be the father of Laura Mance's unborn child. He had felt the anger one feels when a fellow countryman behaves badly.

Lu knew better than to stereotype all Americans, but he was convinced that many were like friendly dogs poking their curious noses into everything without fear and responding with lively enthusiasm at the first sign of intimacy. For most Chinese, this openness was both a source of envy and a reason for disdain. Americans were difficult to understand. Of course, the freedoms that Americans had probably made them less cautious than the Chinese whose history had taught them to weigh every word and every action. He knew that Americans often considered the Chinese to be passive. They weren't so much passive as fearfully prudent. Sometimes they overcame that fear and behaved with extreme bravery, but, for the most part, they persevered in their ordinary activities with the shadows of events such as Tiananmen lying somewhere on the edge of their consciousness. The worst thing was that the *turmoils* seemed to be cyclical. Only the young were unaware of that. It was they who felt immortal.

Lu set the cup down with a determined clunk, checked to see that Rachel had finished, then said, "Let's go."

Laura was in the corner of the compartment leaning against a stack of pillows. Frank sat next to her holding her hand in his. He quickly pulled away as Rachel and Lu Xing entered the compartment. With a deliberate gesture, Laura reached out and replaced his hand over hers looking straight at Rachel and Lu as she did so. The sight of the small white fingers resting under Frank's tawny hand made Rachel's heart ache for the vulnerability of these two young people.

Lu turned to Claire saying, "Thank you for your help. Perhaps now you can return to your compartment please."

As soon as Claire left, Frank spoke with a definite firmness, "We would like to stay together."

114

Lu Xing waved a gesture of dismissal indicating that it would be all right. He looked at Laura and said bluntly, "Are you going to have the baby?"

She flinched at his words but didn't respond. Rachel could see Frank's hand tighten over hers. Lu Xing continued as though he had received his answer from the movement.

"Mrs. Mance, was Sidney Mance the father?"

Laura's eyes grew wide. She stared at Lu Xing as though mesmerized. Then she looked at Rachel with an expression which was more pleading than accusing. She shook her head no. A tear ran down her left cheek. Still staring, she absently flicked it away with her hand. Frank glared at the detective.

"Mrs. Mance, did you have reasons to kill your husband?"

The tears began to flow rapidly down Laura's face. "No, no never to kill!" She collapsed into hiccuping sobs.

Feeling unable to do anything, Rachel looked intensely at her shoes as Lu proceeded to press inexorably on with his questions. Until that moment, Frank had been sitting wrapped in the stillness that Rachel had come to recognize in her Chinese students as a cover for intense agitation. Suddenly that agitation erupted into an angry torrent of staccato Chinese directed at Lu Xing.

Lu sat motionless under the assault. When Frank Li had finished speaking, the tension seemed to ebb from his body. Lu Xing responded saying simply, "*Wo dong.*" (I understand.)

Rachel was amazed at the change in Lu Xing's demeanor. Whatever Frank had said had convinced Lu that Frank was not a reprehensible person, but was, obviously, one who very much loved Laura Mance.

Lu paused to think for a moment, then he said, "Nevertheless, you would, I suggest, have much to gain at the death of Sidney Mance."

Frank Li responded with a straightforward, "Yes." But now there was no anger in his voice.

Laura leaned forward. Her wan face was so pale that her hair seemed to have darkened and taken on an added intensity. The skin was drawn tightly over the bones in her face making the impression her fragile beauty gave even stronger. She seemed to take on the agitation that Frank had rid himself of. She spoke with a quiet forcefulness. "I'm the one who initiated things. I'm the one at fault. I hadn't realized how unhappy I was with Sidney until I met someone who respected me as a person completely separate from himself. I was afraid it would never happen again. I couldn't lose it. It was the rest of my life I was thinking about. Nothing else mattered. I knew how Frank felt, but I also knew he would never say anything. It was the only thing I could do if I cared about myself. I convinced him that we should be together, and I will never be sorry for that."

Lu said, "It seems as though you, too, had much to gain if your husband died. You could marry Frank; The two of you could go to the United States; you would inherit a prosperous business."

Laura looked defeated. "You're right, of course, and sometimes I imagined Sidney just disappearing — how much easier it would be. I even thought of him dying in a plane crash or something, but these were all just fantasies which I knew wouldn't happen. I don't know how to convince you. I must seem like an awful person, but you must believe me. I didn't even think of killing him. I was able to commit adultery; I couldn't possibly have lived with murder."

"What had you planned to do about the baby?" Rachel asked.

"Oh, we'd gone over and over what our possibilities were. I'm not sure that Sidney would have consented to a divorce. Naturally, I could get one eventually without his consent, but that would have meant going back to the U.S. to live for some time without Frank. There was no way we could think of to get Frank there without us being married. We had decided that I would ask Sidney for a divorce. If he wouldn't agree, I would return to the United States just long enough to have the baby. My mother doesn't know yet. She'll be angry at first, but she'll help, and she'd never forgive me if she couldn't be near when her first grandchild was born. I would have taken the time to settle my affairs in the States. Then I would have returned to China with our child to live with Frank and hope that things would change in the future."

Rachel looked dubious. "Do you really believe you could have been happy living here? It's so different from what we're used to.

It's not just the lack of comfort. Going without electricity part of the time, having hot water only some of the time and not having our own cars is something of an adventure for a year or so, but to consider it forever seems pretty grim. There are so many other things you'd miss, places, events, foods ..."

Laura smiled wryly, "Don't think I didn't consider all the problems. Just learning the language well enough to live here forever seemed an impossible thing." She turned to Frank and smiled. "But I could have done it; we could have done it. Now things are different, but what Frank will have to do will be just as hard. Whichever way, we'll make it work."

She paused for a moment, then continued. "I haven't forgotten that Sidney is dead. He was my husband. There were a lot of good things about him. He was intelligent and could be charming and funny when he wanted to be. We had shared many happy moments. You can't just wipe those away. I *am* sorry that he is dead. There were so many things he wanted, so many things he should have been able to do. When I made up my mind to leave him, I was able to begin looking at him more dispassionately. I was able to appreciate what was good about him as a human being. I guess I can't do more than that." She compressed her lips and began to cry again, quietly.

Rachel reached over and patted her lightly on the shoulder. She could see that Lu Xing disapproved of the gesture, but she couldn't stand back and treat Laura like an ordinary suspect. She would stake her life on it; neither Laura nor Frank was the killer.

"We know you were in the dining car when Long Qiong was assaulted," said Lu Xing, "but where were you during the time Sidney was murdered?"

Laura and Frank looked at each other to determine who should answer. Through some sort of unspoken accord Laura began.

"We were together most of the time. We'd been talking over when the best time might be for me to approach Sidney about the divorce. I knew he would be angry. I thought it would be best to do it here on the train where there would be other people to intervene. Ironically, I expected that it would be safe on the train."

117

Frank spoke up. "I didn't think she should do it alone. I thought we should wait until we were in Jilin. Then we could both talk to him in his apartment. We hadn't agreed on what we would do — at least I thought we hadn't. I went to the attendants' compartment to get some hot water for tea just before Sidney was killed."

Laura interrupted him, "Yes, but when he left, I suddenly made up my mind. I couldn't stand the uncertainty one minute longer. I didn't want Sidney to be able say the kinds of nasty things to Frank that I knew he would, so I decided right then to talk to him alone. I had just opened the door of the compartment Frank and I were in when we went through another tunnel. I stood in the doorway until the train started out of the tunnel. Then I went to talk to Sidney." She shuddered. "I found him ... the way he was."

"I see," said Lu. "I'm glad you have been honest. Someone had seen Frank at the other end of the car right before the murder. I knew you weren't together. Mrs. Mance, what can you tell me about your husband's employees, George Kim and Claire Lucas?"

"I know Sidney was very pleased that George was picking for him. He said that George must have been born knowing what was good. Sidney couldn't understand it. He thought it was a fluke, the way some people can see whole pages of copy in their minds — some kind of an ability a person just has. We didn't see Kim socially, if that's what you mean, so I don't really know him very well. Now, Claire I like. Sidney had a strange sort of relationship with her. Sidney pretended there was no problem, but something must have happened that I don't understand. Nevertheless, Claire and I occasionally spent some time together — you know, having lunch — wandering around Chinatown — sometimes even going to the movies. I do know that Sidney couldn't have run the gallery without her. She is a very competent person."

At that point, Rachel asked impulsively, "You realize that the gallery will be yours now. What will you do with it? Will you keep Claire and George on?"

Laura looked surprised. She said, "I guess I didn't even think about the business — only how Sidney's death affected me person-ally, I mean with Frank. Yes, I suppose I would like to continue the gallery, especially if Claire would stay on. And of course if George would continue ... yes, that would be all right, but it's so strange to be talking about this. It will take a while ..."

She looked at Frank for confirmation of what she had decided. He said, "Whatever you want. I will help, but we must get through the problems here first."

Lu agreed. "There will be much to do even when we do find the murderer. Formalities, papers, ah ..." he said with a dispirited sigh. "Can you think of anything else which could help our present difficulties?"

Laura reflected for a moment. "Sidney did seem preoccupied lately, but also rather, ... I'm not sure ... I guess euphoric would be the best word."

Lu looked to Rachel for help.

"Exceedingly happy — feeling quite good," she supplied.

"But do you know why?" asked Lu.

"No, but I don't think it had anything to do with a woman. I think it was something to do with the gallery. I'm sorry. I just don't know."

"There were many women?"

"Yes," Laura replied looking down at her hands, "I'm afraid so."

"Anything else?" queried Lu glancing first at Laura and then at Frank. Both of them just shook their heads, no.

"I will need to talk to you later," said Lu, "but for now, we will leave you."

Frank asked, "Just what are you looking for?"

Lu let out a long breath. "I wish I knew." He and Rachel returned to their compartment. As far as Rachel could see, they were no further ahead. She gave Lu an inquiring look. He merely gazed out of the window and began to recite:

A Death-Blow is a life-blow to some

Who, till they died, did not alive become;

Who had they lived, had died, but when

They died vitality began.

"Emily Dickinson, no doubt," thought Rachel in an exceedingly bad humor, "*whatever* in the world he means by quoting that!"

A glum silence descended in their compartment.

Chapter 17

Claire stood in the doorway looking with hesitation at Rachel and Lu Xing.

"Please sit," said Lu motioning to the seat opposite him. "We will speak English to convenience Rachel Laoshi. She will help me question. You were where when Long Qiong was assaulted?"

Rachel interposed, "I can tell you that myself. She and George were talking on the platform on the other side of the toilet. Right, Claire?"

Claire nodded yes.

"And before Mance was murdered — before the second tunnel?" added Lu Xing.

"Oh, George and I were together in our compartment," she said in an offhand way.

"George Kim and you are good friends?" questioned Lu further.

"Yes, we've know each other for some time."

"This *some time* is how long?" asked Lu.

"About two years, I'd say."

Rachel asked, "Do you see each other only at the gallery or do you meet outside the gallery also?"

Claire shot her a *none of your business* look but then answered in an even voice devoid of emotion. "We are lovers."

Lu looked surprised. George Kim had told them as much, but Lu hadn't expected Claire to be so open about it. American women certainly were different. He was not sure what to ask next; however, Rachel saved him by changing the direction of the questioning. She said abruptly, "Tell us about your relationship with Sidney Mance."

"Strictly business." Claire said in a clipped tone of voice. "My mother and I both worked for his father for a good many years."

"And did your mother also work for Sidney?" Rachel asked.

"No." Claire replied with a decided emphasis.

"What did your mother do working for Sidney's father?" Lu Xing said.

"Actually she did about everything there was to do around a gallery. She kept the financial books, handled the correspondence, arranged for special gallery shows and hired the personnel to install them. She also maintained the day to day sales. Even though her English wasn't very good, Sidney's father, Randolph Mance, recognized her ability immediately. In the later years, she even negotiated the purchase of many of his art works. Mr. Mance was wonderful to both of us. And my mother was indispensable to the gallery."

"Rachel *Laoshi* told me that you had a stepfather who was an American. What about him?" questioned Lu Xing.

"I really don't see that these questions are relevant," Claire snapped.

Lu looked unperturbed. He responded, "Please answer as a help and a kindness to me. Something you say may be important. Your stepfather ...?"

Claire studied him for a moment, and then decided to cooperate. "He died of lung cancer only a few years after we returned to the States. He didn't leave much money, so my mother had to look for work almost immediately. It was hard when she was so new to the country. She tried for days without success. She told me that on one particular day, when she had met with a number of rejections, she decided to take a different route home down a street which had a row of antique shops and art galleries on it. She had been fascinated by American cowboys ever since we had arrived in America. She stopped outside the Mance Gallery to look at one of the Remingtons in the window. She must have seemed especially vulnerable. When Randolph Mance noticed her admiring the Remington in the gallery window, he went outside to invite her in to look. They talked, and he hired her right then to do odd jobs around the gallery. In no time, she was reorganizing the place."

Rachel looked puzzled. "You said Remington. I though the Mance Gallery dealt strictly in Asian art."

"It does now," replied Claire, "but when it was run by Randolph Mance, it dealt mostly in American art. I know it seems incongruous that my mother, a Chinese woman, should be drawn to and have such a good eye for American art, but for some reason she did.

The gallery had a number of pieces of sculpture by Frederic Remington; it sold watercolors by Winslow Homer and James Whistler. It was one of the first galleries to have a sizable collection of San Ildefonso and Santa Clara pottery. We had a good collection of works of Maria Martinez. Most of those have been sold now."

"So how ...?" Rachel began. Lu Xing was looking as though he didn't understand everything, but he was afraid to interrupt.

"Sidney," Claire said. "As soon as his father died ...
I had met Sidney only once. Randolph Mance and his wife had separated when Sidney was a child. Sidney lived somewhere in the East with his mother. He got his education there, Carnegie Mellon, I believe, and was teaching art at a small liberal arts school in Pennsylvania at the time of his father's death. Sidney inherited everything," Claire paused. "Everything."

Rachel looked at Lu Xing. She must keep Claire talking. She sensed that Claire would shut down once she stopped. Rachel asked hastily, "How did you come to be working for Sidney Mance, then?"

There was a slight hesitation before Claire answered as though she were forming the replies carefully in her mind. "Actually, I began working for Randolph Mance when I was in high school. As I told you, my mother had started to handle all the correspondence of the gallery. Even though my mother insisted that I study Chinese with her so that I could read, write and speak it; I had been educated in the U.S., and my English was very good. Her's wasn't. I edited all her letters. I ran errands for the gallery and did many of the simpler things that a teenager could do. That was a wonderful time. Mr. Mance was like family to us. When I graduated from high school, he paid for my education at a nearby business college. Gradually, I learned some of the intricacies of the gallery work so that my mother, who was getting older, didn't have to work such long hours. When Sidney Mance inherited the gallery, he asked me to stay on."

Lu interposed, "But not your mother?"

"No." Again in the clipped voice.

Rachel thought to herself, "Now is the time to gamble on what George Kim said when we interviewed him." She said to Claire, "Tell us about the trouble between Sidney Mance and your mother."

Claire looked stunned. "How — how ... ?" she faltered. "Not George? Surely he wouldn't have told you about that."

Rachel tried not to look at Lu Xing as she plunged on. "But he did. He told us quite a bit about it, but perhaps his version is not quite correct. Hum?"

Claire began to shake. "Damn, damn. How could he? All right, what he probably told you was true. Mother and Sidney had a horrible argument. Randolph Mance had promised my mother several pieces from the gallery as he said, 'for her retirement nest egg.' There was a very valuable Winslow Homer which he had removed from the salesroom early on and had hung in mother's office because she said she was fond of it. He told her it was hers. There were a number of fine pots and a few other pieces— some excellent paintings. All in all, they would have made her life easy for the rest of her days, if she chose to sell even a few of them. Randolph Mance had also been drawing up documents to make her a partner in the gallery. She was that good."

"But . . ?" said Lu Xing.

"But the promises weren't put into writing. Randolph Mance died, and Sidney wouldn't honor any of his father's wishes. I guess my mother went a little crazy. She took the painting and the pots. They were hers. They were!" Claire's voice rose.

"What happened then?"

"Sidney had no idea how to run the gallery. He didn't want my mother there, but he wanted the art work back that she had taken, and he needed someone to run the gallery. He told me he would not press charges against my mother if I would agree to stay to supervise the gallery. I also had to agree that when my mother dies, I will return the things she took. I felt trapped. I didn't know what to do," Claire said simply. "I agreed."

"And your mother?" Lu said.

"When Sidney discovered that she had taken the things his father had promised her, he confronted her. There was a horrible scene." Claire paused. Her brow wrinkled.

"What happened?" asked Lu Xing.

"She had a stroke. I blame Sidney. He destroyed her. She is no longer the strong woman who was my mother. She is like a child whom I don't even know. I pleaded with him to let her keep the things she had taken. I knew it would kill her if she had to give them up. That's how we came to the agreement that I will return them when she dies."

"I see," said Lu, "I see."

"No you don't really. Sidney has used the situation to play games with me. He needed me to run the gallery, and he enjoyed knowing that I was afraid for my mother. It's been horrible."

"So you had reason to hate Sidney Mance." Rachel said more as a statement rather than a question.

"Yes, I did hate him, so I guess that makes a good case for me as a suspect, but, whatever you might think, I didn't murder him. I couldn't."

Rachel looked at Claire with sympathy. Sidney had assuredly mastered the knack for making enemies.

Lu continued as though he hadn't heard Claire's denial. "George Kim explained his working relationship with Mance when we interviewed him, but you may be able to tell us more. George said you told him one time that Mance had lied to him about the selling price of a piece which George had found for him. He said that Mance paid him much less than the 40 percent they had agreed to. Is that true? And were there other times?"

"No, just the once. You see, I do, did, the books for the gallery. I knew what the selling price was. I knew Sidney had tried to cheat George."

"And you told George."

"Yes, I told him. By then I thought we ... George and I ... I thought, that is, George is much younger than I am, but I though it would work between us."

"What happened when George found out?" asked Lu.

"Naturally, he confronted Sidney. They had a terrible fight. George threatened to quit finding things for Sidney. Of course Sidney knew that George is really good at *picking*, so he paid him what he owed. After that, George checked with me on every sale."

"*Picking* is what?" asked Lu.

"In the antique business, owners of the business often just don't have the time to search for things to sell. That is where the *picker* comes in. He or she finds the antiques and sells them to the dealer. Some dealers have a number of *pickers*. I think Sidney was hoping that Laura would learn enough Chinese for him to send her here as his *picker*, keeping it all in the family so to speak."

"Ah, I understand." said Lu. "And Sidney was angry that you told George?"

"Of course, but our relationship, Sidney's and mine, had achieved a kind of balance. He needed me. I could challenge him on his dealings. He knew I was honest and was meticulous about keeping the gallery dealings straight. It amused him. He knew he had a hold over me, so he was willing to concede on a number of things. Strangely, I think he liked having me work for him even though he knew how strongly I felt about him. It gave him a sense of power. He didn't even treat me as though I were Chinese. I guess that's because I'm such a *banana*."

Both Rachel and Lu Xing looked startled. Lu said, "*Banana*, what is it meaning?"

Claire laughed for the first time during the interview. "It's what some Chinese call another Chinese person who is so Americanized that she's yellow on the outside but white on the inside." She smiled broadly showing her beautiful white teeth.

Lu Xing just shook his head.

"You know it's strange," Claire continued. "Sidney was crazy about Chinese art, but I don't think he liked the people who made it very much." With that pronouncement, she looked sober again.

"How long would you have continued to work for Sidney?" Rachel asked.

Claire shrugged. "I tried not the think about it — until my mother died I suppose. Then I would have given the things back and been done with him. I'm very good at running the galley and I'm proud of the place. I am well paid, and Sidney was gone a lot. It seemed like my gallery then. It was only when he was around that things sometimes were intolerable. It could have been worse."

Lu Xing looked thoughtful. "You are the expert on Chinese art, correct?"

"Not really, I know when something is good, but I don't know its actual value. George is the expert. He's had no schooling, but he's absorbed it by osmosis."

"Osmosis is what?" asked Lu.

"Like a sponge gathering up water." said Rachel.

Lu dutifully wrote this in the margin of his notebook. "You said you made Mance be honest in the gallery. Was he always honest?"

"Well, there was nothing illegal with the gallery finances. I made sure of that. But George often brought things into the country for Sidney without paying duty and without papers. I'm sure that Sidney used the nontaxable aspect of his foundation, *Teachers for a New World,* to his advantage when it came to personal taxes, but I didn't do those taxes, only the gallery's."

"What about Mrs. Mance?" inquired Lu Xing.

"What do you mean? As far as honesty goes? I know Sidney was unfaithful to her numerous times. I'm sure she wasn't aware of the kind of person he actually was. I like Laura, and we get along well. We sometimes do things together — go to other gallery openings, the movies — she doesn't know what Sidney did to my mother, and somehow I felt that if I told her, it would change her feeling toward me — you know, make her self-conscious. I enjoy her. None of it was her fault."

"Is there anything else you can tell us?" Lu asked.

Claire looked uncomfortable for a moment, but she shook her head. "No, I don't thinks so," she said.

Lu stood up and opened the door of the compartment. "Thank you for talking with us," he said as he ushered her out. "I will probably want to talk to you again. Please think about the most recent events."

When Claire had left the compartment, Lu Xing looked at Rachel with a sad smile. "So, we get closer," he said. Claire Lucas does not now have the difficult employer; moreover, she and her mother may be able to keep the valuable things. A strong motive, correct?"

"But I don't think strong enough. Somehow I just can't imagine her killing him that way." Rachel replied. "I do think there are things that she didn't tell us — about Sidney's business dealings — about George Kim — I don't know. I just have the feeling she was trying to hide something."

"Most possibly," Lu said knowingly. "Most possibly."

Chapter 18

Long Qiong could no longer stand being in his compartment doing nothing. His head ached, and he was in an agony of indecision. His brother, Wenshi must have known about the vase. If not, why, then, was he on the train? Qiong was sure it had been Wenshi who was peering into the compartment earlier. He must find him and talk to him. But how? Lu Xing have given orders that Qiong was to remain in this car. If it was Wenshi who had hit him over the head and stolen the vase, why was Sidney Mance dead? It didn't make sense.

Who else knew the vase existed? George Kim, of course, and Mance and Mance's secretary, Claire Lucas. Did Mance's wife know? Probably not. She hadn't seemed to know much about her husband's business dealings; although she did know about Chinese art. Long Qiong remembered her keen interest in the art of the old Buddhist and Daoist temples they had visited. Rachel Toussant also seemed to be more knowledgeable about Chinese art than he would have expected her to be. He wondered idly if most visiting foreign teachers studied the art of China before coming to teach. More to the point for that matter, he speculated about what Wenshi, who had scorned a classical education, knew about such things. If he somehow knew about the vase, would he have known that it had such great value? Probably — Wenshi was no fool.

He had to talk to Wenshi. He was sure that once they had spoken together, he would know whether Wenshi had the vase or not. If he were somehow involved in Mance's death, Qiong must protect him. He *was* family. He *was* his brother.

Qiong left his compartment to find Lu Xing who was seated with Rachel Toussant at the end of the car in the compartment which had belonged to the military men. Qiong went in and sat down beside Lu.

"I must talk to you." Qiong spoke directly to Lu in Chinese.

Lu inclined his head but did not reply. If he remained silent, perhaps Long Qiong would become uncomfortable enough to tell them what he was hiding. Rachel took her cue from Lu and was also silent.

Qiong cleared his throat and began, "There is something I must know. I cannot find out if I must stay in this car. I give you my word that I will not try to leave the train. I give you my word that I did not murder Sidney Mance. You must let me have a little time."

Lu Xing pondered this unusual request. Long Qiong was low on his list of suspects. He was fairly sure that the blow to Qiong's head had been severe enough to prevent him from having the strength or the clarity of mind to so quickly and efficiently kill Mance. Lu was just as certain that Long Qiong knew very well why he had been attacked. He possessed the missing piece of the puzzle which, when restored, would make everything clear. If, by granting Qiong's request, he could get him to reveal the motive for the attack, he should be able to find the murderer. They would soon run out of time. The sky was almost dark; they should be arriving in Jilin soon. It was worth a chance.

Lu looked at Rachel. He relayed to her what Qiong had requested. She gave her agreement with a slight inclination of her head. "All right," he said. "I will tell the attendants that you may move through the train free. I expect you to return here soon as possible. I believe you know why you were attacked. When you return, I want the reasons."

Lu spoke to the car attendants. Qiong was free to go.

When he had left, Rachel turned to Lu and asked, "Lu Xing, what will happen to the murderer?"

"That very depends. If he is a Chinese, he will be shot in the back of the head. If he is American — hah, then I will have great *nighthorses*."

Rachel didn't even blink. "Nightmares," she corrected absently, "and no *very* in front of depends." She pictured the small, precise hole at the base of the skull. She had seen posters in Jilin advertising the public execution of criminals in the local parks. The thought made her shudder.

"Why mares, not horses?" Lu asked.

"I really don't know," she answered automatically. "I'll have to find out."

Lu's words had triggered her memory so that, unbidden, she was caught up in a scene she and her fellow teachers had witnessed on the day before Christmas.

They had gone downtown in Jilin to buy last minute supplies and gifts for the Christmas celebration they were holding together that evening. Laughing excitedly, they had boarded a bus to return to the university. They were immersed in a newfound sense of the holiday. Somehow it was much more meaningful in China out of the context of all the commercial fanfare which would have attended the month preceding Christmas in the West. They were reinventing the celebration of a momentous event, and because of that re-invention, were most mindful of its significance. Whether they believed literally in the powerful story as many did, or believed that it was a metaphor for the miraculousness of life, they all felt the awe of the event.

In the midst of this mood, a strident, female Chinese voice blared out over a loudspeaker. Their bus and all the many people on bicycles pulled to the side of the road and stopped. A convoy of open-bed trucks advanced down the center of the highway toward them. The harsh voice came in an endless litany from a uniformed woman in the cab of the lead truck.

The sun fell with a sparkling, brittle harshness on the heads of the people the voice denounced. They were prisoners standing huddled together against the 20 degree below zero winds which swept through the backs of the open trucks. Many had placards hanging around their necks describing the crimes they had committed. Most hung their heads in shame and shivered from the cold and from fear, but a few defiantly braved the bitter wind and stood erect with an almost regal demeanor. Rachel was reminded of the sketches of the royal prisoners of the French Revolution which pictured them as they went to their executions in tumbrels through the streets of Paris.

She and her friends had asked one of the Chinese passengers on the bus what was to happen. They were told that the truck would make a two or three-hour circuit of the city before taking the prisoners, who were to be killed, to the park for a public execution.

The idea was to also shame the family of those who had committed the crimes by making a public example of the criminals.

The scene had stayed in all of their minds as they tried to celebrate what, for them, should have been a holy time. Rachel would always see the unblinking eyes and the upright resolve of one of the women in the second truck. Rachel wondered what she had done, and she wondered what sustained her.

Rachel and Lu sat in silence. Both were deep in thought. Lu was reviewing what they had learned so far. He could come to no conclusions. No, none, now it all depended on what Long Qiong did — on what Long Qiong said.

Lu dreaded the prospect of contacting the American Embassy in Shenyang to report the murder of an American and to arrange for the transfer of the body. The complexities of what he would have to do made his mind reel. If Sidney had been murdered by an American — .. but it might be even worse if he had been murdered by a Chinese citizen. Lu couldn't bear to think about that aspect of the case any longer. He realized that he was getting hungry. If he were only at home now with his wife sitting down to an uneventful dinner.

"Rachel *Laoshi*."

"umh, Yes?"

"My wife cooks food well. When we solve this crime, I will have you eat dinner. OK?"

"To dinner, to dinner," she replied absentmindedly. Suddenly, she looked up. "What if it was Sidney who hit Long Qiong? What if Long Qiong had something valuable that Sidney wanted?"

" I had thought of that," responded Lu. "But why wouldn't Long Qiong tell us that?"

Rachel looked dejected, "I don't know. But there might be good reasons."

"There were many reasons to kill Sidney Mance, but we are no closer to who. We must wait. Long Qiong is the answer."

Rachel picked up the diagrams of the compartment with the positions of the occupants laid out. Maybe if she studied them long enough, the answer would pop out at her. Sometimes things worked that way.

Lu Xing began to flip through his notebook with the same thought in mind. Was there anything he had overlooked? Both of them tried to guess the purpose of Qiong's request. Both of them tried to imagine what he was doing.

As Qiong hurried through the cars, he could hear snatches of gleeful conversation.

"The Americans are killing each other in their train car."

"What is so unusual about that?" someone replied. "I know for a fact that it happens all the time on their television. My cousin in Taiwan told me. He has a large color TV. He says murder is common among Americans."

"Yes, they are very difficult people to understand." said another passenger.

The hard-seat cars were filled with travelers crammed together on row after row of wooden benches. Bluish, smoke hung heavily in the air, and the smell of all manner of foods which had been kept too long in the heat made Qiong nauseous. He scanned the heads looking for one which was alone, one which was familiar.

In the third car forward, he saw him. Wenshi was leaning in the corner with his arms curled around his head shamming sleep. Long Qiong stepped across several noisy passengers and grabbed him by the front of his coat hauling him to his feet. The other passengers grumbled at Qiong as he pulled Wenshi into the aisle and out onto the connecting platform between cars, but no one interfered. Even Wenshi did not resist.

As soon as the doors swung closed on the car, Wenshi whispered urgently, "What has happened to the vase?"

Long Qiong loosened his hold in surprise. "You knew! You don't have it?"

"I swear, my brother, I do not have it."

"How long have you known?" asked Long Qiong.

"Since you and our mother brought it into the house. It is very beautiful; isn't it?"

Long Qiong was astounded. Wenshi had known all this time and done nothing to interfere. Surely, then he would not have tried to get it now. Qiong questioned his brother further. "You saw it? How?"

133

"Behind the cooking pots is not the most intelligent place to hide something of value," he responded in an amused way.

"Why did you follow me to Yanji? Why were you looking into the compartment?" Long Qiong demanded.

"I guessed what you wanted to do. Your son — my nephew, Long Fu — I worried. The vase is very valuable. We are family. I should have been able to help you protect it. I have failed."

"I thought I knew you, Wenshi — always for yourself — always ready to follow your precious Chairman Mao to destroy the old. Why should I believe that you have changed?"

"Long Qiong, I *am* older. Mao was wrong. Once you destroy the old, the connections, there is only yourself and the state left. And the state has become as corrupt as it ever was before the Revolution. Even I can see that. As for myself," here Wenshi gave an ironic grimace, "my self has become harder and harder to live with as I grow older. Oh, I've been angry about the vase. Why should it be your secret just because you're the older brother? What good is something of value if it just stays hidden year after year? You would have known me better if we had talked as brothers do. I admit, I've thought about stealing it and trying to sell it, but I wouldn't know who to contact. I would surely be cheated. I must confess, I could have stolen it from you easily, but I could not steal from our mother, no, not from our mother.

Now you say it is gone. I suspected as much when I heard you were attacked — stolen just when it could be of some use to buy Long Fu's freedom if he is alive. Even now, if someone handed it to me, I might be tempted to take it and disappear. But I know I wouldn't be able to live with myself if I did. I don't have it. I swear on our father's grave. Let me help you get it back. Permit me to buy my way back into our family by doing this thing." He began to weep.

Long Qiong had not seen Wenshi cry since he was about three years old when, together, they had witnessed a band of older boys, who were foraging for food, savagely attack and kill a stray dog. It had been necessary for Long Qiong to drag Wenshi home to keep him from interfering and possibly being harmed by the angry boys. Wenshi had gone to bed that night without eating. After that incident, Long Qiong had never seen him show fear. He became more like the wild boys than like the Wenshi whom Qiong had known.

Long Qiong embraced him roughly. He spoke in a choked voice, "I am glad to truly have you in the family again. We must think together and plan. I believe you. It must have been Sidney Mance who took the vase. He decided to steal it rather than buy it from me. He gambled on the chance that I would not want to let others know about it. He must have been murdered because he had it."

"Who else knew about it?" asked Wenshi.

"I'm not sure. The Chinese-Korean who first contacted me, George Kim — also Mance's assistant, a woman named Lucas. But who else, I don't know — maybe Mance's wife. I must tell the train detective. He's been questioning people; he may have learned more."

Putting his hands on Wenshi's shoulders, Long Qiong said, "I will count on you my brother to watch. We are near Jilin. When the train stops, get out — away from me — and watch the people in our car as they leave. If one of them does something strange, follow that person. We must get the vase back." He looked Wenshi squarely in the eyes and said softly, "I need your help little brother. Please don't fail me."

Wenshi nodded his understanding. Qiong turned and began to walk swiftly to his car to find Lu Xing, the train detective.

Chapter 19

After being questioned by Lu Xing and Rachel, Claire left the compartment in a daze. Why had she talked so much? When she heard that George had told them about her mother, her pent up feelings had just poured out. Now she was left to explore the implications of George's betrayal. She had to look at things honestly, no matter how painful they might be. She finally realized that she had wanted him to be a certain kind of person, so she had overlooked many things in order to fit him into her preconceived idea of what the man she loved should be.

There had been a number of other men before, but somehow it had never worked; she really wasn't too sorry when it didn't. Until the death of Randolph Mance, her life had seemed close to ideal. She loved her work; consequently, she had always blamed the failure of her romances on the fact that the current man in her life had not been willing to share in her total involvement with the gallery. Often, the person she had been seeing resented the fact that, for her, her mother and the gallery had come first.

With George it had been different, or so it seemed. He, too, was involved with the gallery. His business trips to China and Korea took him away so often that the resentment was more likely to be on her part. The lack of steadiness in their relationship had only whetted her appetite making their time together seem very precious. She was no longer young. George had appeared to be a last marvelous chance which fate had offered her.

He hadn't minded talking about business with her. Naturally not. Hadn't it been to his advantage to do so? What an idiot she was! After all, she had provided him with the probable selling price on each antique he had brought to Sidney. And what about the latest antique George had located in Jilin, the one she had prepared the correspondence for with Long Qiong? She hadn't told George about the contents of Sidney's letters to Long Qiong. Why not? She must not have been as committed to George as she thought. Subconsciously, she must have suspected that George didn't love her all that much.

He would certainly have wondered what had become of his marvelous lead: yet he hadn't said anything to her. She stopped abruptly. She needed to think this out carefully. With shaking hands, she pulled out the jump-seat in the aisle and sat down facing the window. She felt faint. Time seemed to compress and no longer behaved according to strict laws. Since she had been in China, she was unsure of who she really was. She had thought she remembered little of Qingdao, but, at times, memories came unbidden as fresh and real as if she were reliving them at that very moment. She had a problem to solve concerning her life now, but all she could think of was herself as a child playing in the muddy streets of Qingdao. She had been totally unaware of the filth which had only become a factor by contrast with her later surroundings. All new experiences had been things of wonder. The beggars in the streets and the occasional corpse she had come upon held no terrors for her. At most, they had been objects of curiosity — things which, at the time, seemed to belong there. For her, as a child, the world had always been that way. Even the adults such as her mother, who lived among the poverty and filth, no longer saw it. War, hunger and exhaustion had numbed them to anything beyond attention to the moment, worry over the next meal, and concern only for those they loved. They didn't notice the dirt which caked their threadbare silk jackets making them stiff and dull. During the day they ignored the blue weals and the black spots on their hands that came in the winter from the constant exposure to extreme cold. Only at night when their minds were disengaged, did they admit to pain and sometimes dream of the splendid holidays of the past with their banquets, firecrackers, candles and torches and the warm, comfortable laughter.

In the midst of this grinding poverty, Claire's first encounter with her future stepfather had been one of suspicion. For her, he was difficult to identify. He had no distinctive smell, no special markings on his clothing such as the stains on her grandfather's trousers, or the many darns in her mother's skirt.

It was only later that she learned that her stepfather represented cleanliness and material comfort from another world. And only later did she look back in wonder at her happiness in what she would later label as a squalid environment of the kind she could not possibly bear as an adult. As long as he lived, her stepfather had continued to be a bland entity to her. He was a kindly man for whom she held no particular affection and one whose presence left no distinctive memories.

Thinking of her stepfather made her realize why she had been so drawn to George. He wasn't bland; he represented her past which she hadn't let go of. Her previous loyalty to him had not so much to do with what he actually was. Rather it had to do with what he symbolized, her Chineseness, her origins.

As the train sped past a stand of trees, the dark surface reflected her image back to her from the glass. She had always prided herself on being realistic. Her face was pleasant and intelligent, but certainly not beautiful. What on earth had made her believe George would find her so, when she could see the plain truth? She must have had doubts. No man as handsome and outgoing as George could travel all over the world, yet save himself for this ordinary woman who stared back at her now. She had suppressed her distrust well, but some small kernel of anger and disloyalty had prevented her from telling him about those letters that Sidney had dictated to Long Qiong. She had been preparing for the moment when she would see George as he actually was. That moment had come when he told Rachel and the detective about her mother. She had just been postponing the pain by not letting that knowledge of him surface. George had been a connection with her past, and she had been afraid to look too closely at that link.

She had to rethink the whole business, the assault on Long Qiong, Sidney's murder. She had been shocked by the murder; consequently, she had distanced herself from it as though it didn't concern her. She guessed that it must have been Sidney who assaulted Long Qiong, and, if he had, she wasn't surprised. Sidney had been an opportunist. Why pay for something if you could steal it?

But she had been so sure that she and George hadn't been part of the equation. They were just onlookers. They had been talking on the platform together when Long Qiong was assaulted; moreover, they had been together in their compartment when Sidney was killed. George was her alibi; she was his. But was she . . ? She deliberately forced herself to reconstruct those moments. George said she had dozed off — for how long? She remembered blinking in annoyance at the light suddenly in her eyes. George had been standing facing her just inside the compartment door. He had a strange expression on his face.

He had been looking at her as though assessing her in some way. Quickly he had said, "You just dozed off in mid-sentence. I thought I'd better let some air through the compartment. Look, I've opened the aisle window and the door."

Then he had brushed his hands over his hair, rearranged the flaps on his jacket pockets and had sat down across from her. Leaning toward her, he had put his hands on either side of her knees. She remembered that his hands had been cold; they trembled slightly. He had looked straight into her eyes and said, "You were telling me about leaving Qingdao when you were a child."

"Was I?" she responded in doubt. She had no memory of talking about Qingdao; however, the thought was immediately driven out of her mind by the ensuing chaos. Bedlam broke loose in the aisle outside their compartment. Sidney Mance had been murdered.

Now, without warning, Claire knew. She *had* been asleep — for some time — long enough for George to have murdered Sidney. No one else knew about the vase. Only Sidney, she and George. She realized that she was freezing; yet she also seemed to herself to be outside of her body — the body which had betrayed her even more surely than George had. She had lied and lied and lied ... to herself. She felt no fear, only an intense anger as she walked rapidly to their compartment. She would confront him. She would know everything. Later she would permit herself to deal with the pain.

The train was slowing down as it entered the outskirts of Jilin. "Less than an hour more," George thought, "and I'll be free to work this out." He was not sorry that he had done what he had, but he was angry with himself. Killing Sidney had been unpremeditated. Unplanned events were always chancy. The impulse and the opportunity had coincided. Claire was asleep. He had looked into the next compartment and saw Sidney sitting alone, admiring his

140

antiques. He was certain that Sidney must have the Ming vase. Sidney would not even have known about it, if it hadn't been for him. His anger had welled up inside him; it coalesced and burst like a red clot behind his eyes. He would not be duped again. At that moment, the train had entered another tunnel. Without even thinking, it was done. It had been so easy to grab the Korean vase on the table and use it as a bludgeon. The open window had made it easy to dispose of. Amazingly, he must have calculated all of that in a split second without even being aware of thinking. It had just happened. The Ming vase had been right there beside Sidney under a pillow. Now it belonged to him — now it belonged to George Kim.

He was fortunate that there were so many people who might get along better in this world without Sidney. There were certainly plenty of motives for the detective and the teacher to ponder. He was also fortunate that the vase was so small. The box that housed it was almost the same size as the dictionary which he had kept in his pocket and which he had so often been seen to use. He had discarded the dictionary and placed the box in his pocket. He was confident that he wouldn't be searched. If Long Qiong hadn't mentioned the vase yet, he wasn't going to.

George's impulse was to move forward in the train so that he could get away from the rest of the group and disappear into the crowd. Instead, disciplining himself, he remained where he was. To move now would look suspicious. His luck had held this far. Surely, it would hold a little longer.

He was gathering up his belongings, bending over the seat with his back to the door, when Claire burst into the compartment. With an amazing amount of force, she spun him around to face her. She searched his face intently for a moment, then said very softly spitting her words out, "You did it, George, didn't you? You murdered Sidney. You used me the way you've done before, and you killed him!"

As she lifted her arm to strike him, he grabbed both of her wrists, twisted her down to the seat and held her there. He stuck his right knee into her pelvis pushing her further into the seat. Then he bent over her and thrust his face within an inch of hers.

"Yes, Claire, such a bright girl, you've figured it out. I killed him, and I can kill you."

She suddenly relaxed and pulled herself up straighter in the seat. She looked at him steadily without fear. "But you can't," she said. "I know you can't." They stayed frozen for a moment like two pieces of sculpture; then he swung his hand across her face in a fierce blow which knocked her to the floor. He turned and swiftly left the compartment without looking back.

Chapter 20

Lu Xing and Rachel were studying the diagram on which they had placed the probable positions of everyone in their car during the time of the murder. The perimeter of the paper was decorated with Lu Xing's jottings of English words and their equivalents in Chinese characters.

Rachel could not resist commenting. "The diagram is beginning to look more like a dictionary than an aid to solving a murder."

Lu Xing frowned and held up his hand as though to command silence. "Dictionary!" he exclaimed. with a look of sudden enlightenment. "You told me that George Kim always carried his dictionary in his pocket, but I removed it from the seat when we questioned him, yet both of his pockets had something in them. I wonder what."

"But Kim couldn't have hit Long Qiong." argued Rachel. "I was with him and Claire on the platform then. Do you think the dictionary is important? Anyhow, both he and Claire said they were together in their compartment when Sidney was murdered."

"But they are lovers. They naturally protect each other. Many people have lied. Possibly they both lied."

"Do you seriously think they might have done it together?"

"Hum, I don't know. It would be certain to be easier that way."

Rachel shook her head from side to side. "I can't believe in your conspiracy idea. In any case, what is the motive? We know that Sidney hadn't been very honorable concerning Claire's mother, and Kim certainly had reason to dislike Sidney, but these motives just don't seem strong enough."

Lu agreed but added, "But there may be more that we haven't found out that would make the motive or motives even stronger."

At that moment, with a flurry of movement, Long Qiong burst into their compartment. Somewhat startled, Lu Xing looked at him and commented to Rachel, "Possibly our motive walks in with Long Qiong."

"My vase," Long Qiong began rapidly in Chinese. "Ah, it is too complicated! I was afraid my brother had stolen it from me.

That's why I pretended that nothing was missing. You see, my brother is also on the train. I didn't know that when I got on, but then I saw him looking into the window of my compartment. I thought he was spying on me. I had to find him to see what he was up to. We just talked. He swears he didn't take the vase, and I believe him. It is a most valuable family heirloom — very, very old. I'm convinced now that Sidney Mance attacked me to get it. I had arranged to sell it to him, so he knew about it. He must have taken it. He had it — he must have had my vase — most possibly that's why he's dead."

Lu kept nodding his head rapidly up and down in encouragement as Long Qiong spoke. Rachel found it difficult to follow the rush of Chinese which was coming from Long Qiong. Lu noticed her puzzled look, and told her succinctly in English, "He had a very valuable vase. Mance took it — a strong reason for someone to murder Mance."

Turning back to Long Qiong, Lu asked, "Who else besides you and your brother knew of the vase?"

"I think only the Lucas woman who helped us arrange a meeting and the man named Kim."

"Had either of them ever seen it?" asked Lu.

Long Qiong shook his head. "No, it was with my mother, near Yanji. She had hidden it long ago. I just recently got it. That was the purpose of this trip. Mance was impatient to see it. He kept asking me, but I continued to put him off. I'm sure he must have figured out that I didn't have it in Jilin. When I made arrangements for him to see it as soon as we had returned from Yanji, he must have realized that I went there to get it. What a mistake! I've been so stupid." Long Qiong slipped down onto the seat in a dejected lump.

The train had slowed down now as it passed through the outlying areas of Jilin. The whistle signaled the approach to the station. Rachel realized that it had been dark out for some time.

Lu rose quickly, galvanized into action by the sound. "Come," he shouted to Qiong. "We must question Kim and Lucas." He motioned urgently to Rachel to accompany them. "Hurry," he cried. "Time moves."

144

Swiftly the three left the compartment emerging into the aisle just as Kim shot out of his compartment at the other end of the car. Kim paused for a second, looked their direction with apprehension, then reading the looks on their faces, dived through the door to the next car.

Rachel, Lu Xing and Long Qiong raced down the aisle. They glanced quickly into Kim's compartment. What they saw caused them to check their pursuit momentarily. Claire Lucas was half sitting, half lying on the floor with her legs curled under her. One arm supported her weight. Tears were streaming over an ugly welt under her left eye and running down her face. Her nose was bleeding profusely.

"It was George!" she cried. "He wasn't with me. I had fallen asleep; he murdered Sidney."

Lu quickly shouted for one of the train attendants to help Claire. Then he urged his companions on towards the door through which Kim had disappeared.

In the hard-seat cars, passengers were jamming the aisles, bending over to retrieve bulky packages, talking noisily and jockeying for positions near the door in order to be among the first ones out. It wasn't in the nature of the average Chinese person to wait for a more orderly departure. Almost without fail, any entrance to or exit from a public conveyance degenerated into a mob scene.

As George Kim desperately elbowed his way through the hardseat car, Wenshi noticed the commotion he was causing and sprang to his feet to pursue him. George freed himself of entanglement and lunged into the next car forward. People angrily swatted at Wenshi as he, too, pushed past them.

Before entering the next car in pursuit of Kim, Wenshi looked back for a second towards the far end of the car and saw Long Qiong, the American teacher and the train detective frantically pushing against an almost solid wall of people. Long Qiong caught his eyes and shouted, "Go, go. stop him!" Wenshi ducked between two people knocking them both off balance. A mahjong set fell from someone's hand. As the pieces scattered over the floor, people bent to retrieve them causing even more disorder. The occupants of the car began flailing at each other in an effort to redress real or imagined injury. Wenshi somehow escaped and began battling through the next car accompanied by the curses of indignant people whom he pushed out of the way. He saw Kim ahead forcing himself through the throng onto the far platform. He heard the angry shouts of the people who were knocked against the metal doorways. The train had slowed, almost to a halt. Kim prepared to jump off.

Chapter 21

Taxis were not much in demand in Jilin, China. Although it was a city of close to one million people, it was also a political backwater, provincial in its customs and its services. If it were not possible to bicycle where one needed to go, then public buses usually had to suffice. These buses were incredibly, slow, dirty and uncomfortable, often being crammed well beyond reasonable capacity; however, they generally got to their destinations sooner or later. Lumbering dinosaurs, they moved vast streams of people slowly back and forth like barges on a river.

Taxis could zip from one side of the city to the other, but the ride could easily consume a tenth of a person's monthly income. Cars were well beyond the reach of the individual, and few people knew how to drive. Each work unit had one or several cars depending upon its importance. These were usually driven by men or women who had learned to drive in the People's Liberation Army. It was not unusual for these drivers to flaunt their importance while trying to terrorize the lone cyclist who might have strayed away from the moving mass of people which clogged the streets day and night.

Still, there were several decrepit taxis in Jilin. They were generally discarded Soviet cars in which hopeful entrepreneurs doggedly waited at the train station for the possible arrival of important cadres or Westerners involved in the ever-growing number of *joint-venture* companies springing up all over China.

As the train from Yanji pulled into the Jilin station, several of these waiting taxis sat scattered among the press of people, bicycles and work unit vans. The vehicles were parked wherever and at whatever angle their drivers thought convenient. Rachel and her fellow Americans had often wondered why strips weren't painted to designate parking places around the train station. They concluded that doing so would have taken the random element out of life and made it too easy.

Now as the train approached the station, the passengers looked out at the throng of people and the assorted vehicles crowded near

147

the exit gates. Before the train had fully stopped, George Kim leaped from the steps and ran through the gate into that sea. His safari jacket flapped wildly as he moved. The Ming vase, nestling snugly in the box inside his right pocket, bounced against his hip as he ran. He attempted to hold it still without slackening his pace. He was all too conscious of the person in pursuit of him only a few yards back. He kicked at a bicycle in his path and, just in time, leaped over another one which had fallen in front of him. He could hear cursing as his pursuer became entangled in the bicycles.

Kim frantically scanned the crowded area until he spotted a taxi which seemed to have a clear path ahead of it and was facing the bridge into the city. He lunged for the door of the taxi, jumped into the front seat, and yelled to the driver. "Go. Drive quickly — across the bridge." He tossed two U.S. twenty dollar bills onto the seat beside the driver.

Pleased to have a fare who didn't even ask the price, the driver took off with a grinding of gears just as Wenshi fell against the trunk of the taxi. As the car surged forward from beneath his hands, he stumbled to his knees in the gravel. He took a moment to catch his breath, then turned and sprinted toward another taxi waiting about a hundred yards away. Panting, he fell into it managing to bark out a command to follow the other taxi across the bridge.

"If I lose him," he though, "I won't know where to look." He was consumed with anxiety. Did the man he was chasing even have the vase? Surely, he must. Once again, he felt the old excitement which had surged through him years ago when he was a Red Guard. It was a purposeful restlessness that he had missed. His body wanted to move faster than the car would take him. He saw the taxi they were following turn left in the distance at the end of the bridge and speed down the road which wound along beside the Songhua River. Good, there were some minor turnoffs to the right along the road, but it seemed most likely that the man he was pursuing would stay on the road for several miles until it came to the point where a number of other main roads converged with it like the spokes of a wheel. The man would have more options that way. If Wenshi could just get close enough to see which way the taxi went at that convergence, he might be able to guess where his quarry was going.

Lu Xing had radioed ahead to the station police in Jilin giving them instructions about the American train passengers and the removal of the body. They would have to deal with that without his help. It was his job to catch the killer. At the station, Lu Xing, Long Qiong and Rachel burst through the gates of the train station ignoring the angry shouts of the attendants who tried to check their tickets. They abruptly halted at the top of the stairs leading to the parking area to search for the university van which was to meet them.

"Look — there!" shouted Rachel pointing to the van at the very left edge of a group of vehicles. She started running toward it. Lu Xing and Long Qiong turned to follow. Qiong's wife, Chan Lumei, was standing by the side of the van waving her arms over her head and shouting something which Long Qiong couldn't understand over the noise of the crowd. She looked even younger and more radiant than she had on their wedding day. Anxiety gripped Qiong's chest. Had she had gone completely mad? Why was she here? He hurried toward her catching her up as she rushed into his arms.

"Long Fu is coming home," she cried. "Xiao Fu is coming home."

"How ... when?" Long stammered.

"I don't know how or why. He was just suddenly released from prison. He sent word by one of his friends. He's weak and is resting in Beijing, but he leaves for Jilin tomorrow night on the evening train."

Qiong was afraid to believe. "Truly?" he said anxiously. "Truly?"

"Yes, truly," whispered Chan Lumei as she nuzzled her head into his shoulder.

Qiong stood there holding her and laughing hysterically as though someone had told him the best joke in the whole world.

Rachel and Lu Xing had reached the van when Lu realized that Long Qiong was not with them. With a flash of irritation, he turned to search for him. He saw him standing with his arm around his wife's shoulder laughing or crying, Lu couldn't tell which, as though he had lost his mind.

"Quick," Lu shouted to Rachel, "we must get them in the van. Remember, Kim knows this area. If we lose him, we may not have another chance."

He and Rachel grabbed the couple's arms and pulled them along. Lu's temper was almost out of control. "I don't understand," he shouted. "Some people are crazy." He roared at the driver of the university van with such imperiousness that the startled man quickly obeyed him, totally forgetting that it was not this stranger who should give the orders but Long Qiong.

The dialogue between Long Qiong and Chan Lumei was in such rapid Chinese that Rachel could not understand it; however, after she heard *Long Fu* and *Beijing* several times, and saw their beaming faces, she concluded that Long Qiong's son had been found.

The half-mile long bridge was now crowded with many other vehicles leaving the train station. As the van swung onto the bridge, Lu Xing strained to catch sight of the two taxis that had left the station ahead of them. He was sure he had seen someone else pursuing Kim and concluded that it must have been Long Qiong's brother. It looked to him as though both taxis had turned left at the end of the bridge to take the road along the edge of the Songhua River. There would be little traffic in that direction because the road led away from the city center. It was just possible that they could still catch Kim. Lu issued more commands to the delight of the driver who had seen several foreign chase films on Chinese TV. Soon the van was weaving crazily in and out of the slower moving traffic. With a daring spin of the wheel, the driver cut in front of several vans and turned left onto the Songhua roadway. Rachel was regretting the lack of seat belts in Chinese vehicles.

Like insects pursuing each other, the two taxis and the van skimmed crazily over the road. The full moon wove in and out among the overhanging branches of the willow trees which lined the river. The road ahead was practically deserted, and the silver gleam of the moonlit river seemed to stream along beside them like a rapidly moving ribbon.

Kim's taxi came to a rocking halt in the center of the converging circle of roads. Suddenly it jerked forward again in an erratic turn and sped rapidly down one of the narrow, dirt *hutongs* or alleyways which met the circle.

Wenshi's taxi pulled into the circle just in time to see the other taxi receding into the warren of small passageways.

"The man must be crazy," he thought. Most of the *hutongs* wound around like interweaving coils, but all ended at Beishan, North Mountain. Wenshi couldn't understand why this man had not taken one of the main roads leading to the west or to the northeast of the mountain. It was impossible to guess what must be going on in his mind. It was incomprehensible; the fleeing man was allowing himself to be boxed in.

But George Kim wasn't thinking rationally. He was consumed by one thought only. If he could get inside the temple gate, he would be safe. Surely *his* nun would take care of him again. When his taxi came to the end of the *hutong*, George jumped out running for the path which led up between the mountains. The gate to the path was locked to prevent vehicles from entering the area at night, but it was easy enough for one person to get around it through the brush on either side. As he raced up the cement path, Kim could hear the screeching halt of the other vehicle. He heard angry shouting and then the sound of running feet lower on the path. He began to panic. His eyes darted to the right and to the left. The temple was at the top of the mountain on the right, but there was a concrete retaining wall to the right of the path which would be impossible to scale. The embankment which rose into the mountain on the left was not as steep. There the wall was not as extensive. He could lose himself in the trees on the mountainside. He scrambled up the side of the embankment heedless of the branches tearing at him. As he fought his way nearer to the top of the mountain, he came to the alarming realization that he would have to cross Broken Back Bridge to reach the temple walls. The crashing of his pursuer in the bushes as he closed in, intensified Kim's fear to the point of frenzy. He felt as though his heart would burst.

Clutching wildly at bushes and tree branches, he pulled himself forward in desperate lurches. The vase in his pocket was forgotten. His only thought was to get to the temple. The high stone walls around the temple complex made it seem as impregnable as a fortress, but Kim remembered, from when he was a boy, the small hole hidden by bushes through which he and his nun had tunneled underneath the wall.

His flight retraced the course of his most malignant dreams — the same nightmare to which he had returned again and again — that horrific vision of his mother's destruction —her beautiful, evil relinquishment into the air. Had he ever left this place? He could no longer be sure.

Chapter 22

A third screech of brakes announced the arrival of the van at the bottom of the mountain. Almost simultaneously, Lu Xing and Long Qiong jumped out. Through the elaborate white gate, they could see the two figures, pursuer and quarry, racing up the path. Long Qiong ordered the driver to stay with the van while Lu Xing gave brusque instructions to Rachel and Chan Lumei to remain in the van with the driver. Immediately, the men set off in pursuit.

The two women sat immobile for an instant looking at each other. Then with a wordless agreement, they also jumped out of the van and ran to the high gates marking the entrance to the path. They hadn't seen how the men had circumvented the imposing gates. They paced in front of the barrier in impatient uncertainty until Chan Lumei discovered a small opening to one side in the thicket. Pushing through the brush, the two women ran to the base of the path on the other side of the gates.

They could see Long Qiong and Lu Xing running along the path, but the other two figures in front of them had disappear. Suddenly, two distant shapes reappeared from among the trees at the top of the mountain. The first man stumbled toward the bridge as his pursuer closed in behind him.

Wenshi caught Kim at the edge of the bridge. As he grabbed the neck of Kim's jacket, Kim jerked himself out of it staggering against the balustrade from the force of the movement. Wenshi tossed the jacket behind him; it sailed in a delicate arc and slowly fell, catching on one of the pillars ranged along the parapet. With the agility of a practiced predator, Wenshi leaped upon Kim. His hands closed around Kim's throat. Desperately, Kim thrust one hand under Wenshi's nose pushing at his face and, with the other hand, clawed at the fingers encircling his throat.

Rachel and Chan Lumei stood at the bottom of the path, transfixed by the scene far above them. Like actors on a moonlit stage, the two figures on the bridge struggled slowly and silently, seeming to move in a stylized pavane for their audience below.

With a burst of strength, Kim kicked Wenshi backwards. Wenshi stumbled, fell to the ground, and then crouching, leapt again towards Kim. The force of Wenshi's vault pushed Kim off balance against the balustrade. Like a man possessed, Wenshi dived at Kim with such strength that Kim's body was thrown backwards out onto the ledge of the stone coping. Wenshi abruptly pulled himself back. For a split second, Kim teetered like a plank on a fulcrum until his flailing arms broke the balance and he fell, doing a slow, tortured somersault into empty space.

George Kim did not scream as he fell. To those below, the scene had the strange quality of a silent pantomime. No one was close enough to hear the words, *mama, mama,* that George cried softly to the night air.

Long Qiong and Lu Xing rushed into the clearing near the edge of the bridge just in time to see one of the two men plunge to his death. The other man was at the far side of the bridge leaning over peering down. He ran to where the jacket had caught on the pillar. For a second he hesitated, but in a moment he was gone. They could hear the pounding of his feet echo down one of the paths at the back of the mountain.

Long Qiong's chest constricted. He felt a hundred emotions at once — his brother — the vase— gone — who had died? He forced himself to look over the railing to the cement below. The figure which lay there was twisted and unrecognizable, but he could tell from the clothing that it was Kim. There could be no doubt that Kim was dead. Qiong saw the two women at the bottom of the path move, as though breaking a trance, and start to run rapidly up the path toward the body. He looked behind him in the direction his brother had gone. Then he looked at Lu Xing.

Lu's face was set in an enigmatic expression. He pulled at his lower lip with a thoughtful air. "It was undoubtedly an accident, or perhaps even suicide," he said. Hearing himself speak reinforced Lu in his official attitude toward Kim's death. "Undoubtedly so," he repeated loudly as though challenging the official powers that be to contradict his judgment. He walked over to the edge of the bridge and retrieved Kim's jacket which hung casually on the pillar as though it had been placed there. He reached into one of the

154

large side pockets of the jacket and pulled out the box which held the Ming vase. Handing the box to Long Qiong, he said, "I believe this belongs to you."

Qiong opened it carefully with shaking hands. The vase lay serenely lodged in the layers of silk. His breath caught in his throat. He held the vase up, turning it slowly. In the bright moonlight, he could see that it was miraculously intact. He stared at it in disbelief. Turning to Lu Xing, he held the vase in front of him. With an eloquent sigh he said, "It is over. Now I must show my wife and my son our treasure, our legacy..." And after a pause, he added to himself, "... and our burden."